FROSTED CROAKIES

SAM CHEEVER

ELECTRIC PROSE PUBLICATIONS

Frosted Croakies

Published by Sam Cheever
Copyright 2019 Sam Cheever

'Tis the season for great folly...walawalawalawalala... ribbit.

It's Christmas time at Croakies. The tree is up. The stockings are hung. And Christmas tunes are turning the atmosphere jolly. After a tumultuous Samhain, I've found my chi again and I'm starting to enjoy the season of love and giving.

Yeah. You probably know how this is going to end.

When Sebille suggests I open the bookstore up to a small holiday party, I foolishly agree. How was I supposed to know that the hobgoblin would decide it would be fun to hide everybody's stuff? Or that we'd be hit with a freak winter storm that confined everybody inside for the duration. Or that a "You're me but who am I?" spell would be released inside the shop, switching everybody's identities and creating general chaos and hysteria?

I could probably deal with all that if it weren't for the fact that my friend, Lea...the one person who could possibly reverse the spell...was ensconced in SB the parrot, with no opposable thumbs for spelling.

And me? Of course, I'm sitting fat and squishy inside Mr. Slimy. Thank goodness Rustin isn't currently in residence, or it would be really crowded in here.

Who spelled my party? What do a pair of Santa's elves have to do with it? And why have old enemies suddenly become new friends? I apparently have a little holiday mystery to solve inside Croakies, and I have no idea how I'm going to solve it with everybody mixed up and some of us human.

Have I told you I hate this season?

Ribbit!

'TIS THE SEASON FOR PURE FOLLY

"*I* definitely need to get my head examined," I groused under my breath.

Passing by carrying a box filled with ornaments, Sebille reached up and flicked me on the temple.

"Ow!"

She narrowed her eyes menacingly. "Stop complaining. It's going to be fun. It's about giving back to your customers. Some of them have been coming to Croakies for years, and they're very loyal."

She was right. I was being a Scrooge. I thought of Mrs. Foxladle and Mr. Peabody, two of my favorite customers. They were the kindest souls in the world, and I did enjoy the idea of thanking them for their loyalty and support over the years.

I tugged the last branch of the artificial tree straight and stepped back, squinting at it with a critical eye. "Does that look crooked to you?"

From his perch on the windowsill, looking out into a snowy Saturday afternoon in December, Mr. Wicked gave me his expert, feline opinion. "Meow."

"Thanks, buddy," I told him.

Sebille straightened up from her box of goodies and gave the tree the once-over. "It looks perfect."

There was a soft rustling noise and I turned back to the tree as Sebille hurried away, saying something about lights. The tree was leaning at least six inches to the right.

"Sebille must need glasses," I said, reaching through the branches and tugging it straight. I jammed the whole thing deeper into the stand and infused it with a wisp of magic to keep it there.

I straightened with a groan and stepped back to get a better view.

"Ribbit," Slimy said from his glass tank.

I glanced his way. "I think it's finally straight, don't you?"

Another soft rustling sound had me whipping back around.

The top third of the tree sagged slowly downward, like a Charlie Brown Christmas tree.

Suspicion flared. "Okay, who's messing with me?"

Giggling ensued from somewhere inside the tree. I hurried around back to catch the culprit, and Hobs flew out of the tree, shooting away from me so quickly he left only a streak of color on the air from the red and white holiday scarf he'd taken to wearing around his neck.

Wicked jumped down from the sill and plodded after his friend.

I should have known. The two of them were inseparable. Where there was a Wicked, there was always a hobgoblin.

Sebille settled another box on the floor. "I think that's it." She looked at the tree, frowning. "You broke it."

I sighed. "It wasn't me, it was Hobs."

"Oh." She grinned.

I was really glad she was enjoying the hobgoblin's antics. I was about ready to put a lump of coal in his stocking. The only thing stopping me was that I feared he'd eat it.

I reached up and tried to straighten the top portion of the tree, but I wasn't tall enough. I struggled for a minute, blowing prickly needles off my face as I strained on the very tips of my tippy toes. I huffed out a frustrated sigh as I failed to seat the section properly back into its center support.

"Here, let me try," Sebille said. She popped into her Sprite form on a burst of white light and fluttered upward, her multi-hued wings beating the air behind her as she sent a soft green glow to bathe the sagging treetop in energy. Prodded by a gentle spurt of magic, the sagging segment surged upward and dropped firmly into the center pipe.

I wiped my sweaty palms onto my jeans. "Thanks, Sebille."

She nodded and pointed to the lights. "Give me the end of that, and I'll attach it to the top."

With her flying around and around the tree, we had the lights in place within only a few minutes. I gave her the lighted angel I'd purchased for the top. She put that into place before she popped back to full size again.

My day was looking better. The hard part was done. "Now, all we need to do is add the ornaments," I told her with a smile.

The front doorbell jingled behind me. I turned around to find Lea and Hex blowing in on a blast of icy air. Lea had her head so deep into her frothy, cream-colored scarf she resembled a turtle trying to retreat into her shell. The lumpy brown coat only enhanced the image. The scarf was ginormous, seemingly wide and long enough to serve as a blanket on a twin-sized bed.

My friend smiled brightly at me as Hex hurried toward the back room, gray tail whipping the air with excitement. "It's not fit for man nor beast out there," she said poetically.

Lea handed me something wrapped in foil that smelled like cinnamon and pumpkin. "Merry almost Christmas."

I took the weighty gift and pulled her into a hug.

A snowflake sifted from her scarf and melted on my nose. "Merry almost Christmas, Lea."

Sebille plugged the lights in and our tree exploded with pulsating color and light.

Lea sighed. "So pretty."

Christmas music suddenly filled the air. I squinted at Sebille. "Did you do that?"

She shook her head.

"It was me, Miss."

Hobs stood near the door between the bookstore and the artifact library, his long-fingered hands clutching a small box inexpertly wrapped in red and green plaid foil with a crooked green bow on top. "I brought you a present."

His oversized, pointed ears twitched with embarrassment and his pale cheeks pinkened.

"That's so sweet," I told him, walking over to retrieve the box from his spidery fingers. "Should I open it now?"

He shook his head. "It's your Christmas spirit, Miss. You must keep it intact until the exact moment when you lose hope for the season."

I wasn't sure what to say to that. It was kind of a mixed message. I finally settled on the obvious question. "What if I don't need to unwrap it?"

His grin made him look positively angelic. Good thing I knew better. "All the better, Miss."

I held the box up to my ears. The music was coming from inside. It sounded like an entire orchestra, the sound amazing. "This is wonderful, Hobs. Where did you get it?"

He held up a chastising finger, rocking it back and forth in censure. "Uh, uh, uh, Miss. Don't look a gift spirit in the mouth."

Or...something like that.

I gave him a hug. "I'll put it under the tree." I took a couple of steps toward the tree and stopped, despair making my skin prickle. "We forgot to get a tree skirt!" I immediately regretted the whiny tone of my voice, but I had no time to go back out and get a skirt. Especially since the stores were ridiculously busy and a little scary at that time of year.

"Here, Naida." Lea came to my rescue. Unwinding the enormous scarf, she dropped to her knees beside the tree and wrapped it carefully around the stand. The result was beautiful.

Tears burned my eyes. "Oh, Lea. Are you sure?"

"Absolutely. I came to help you get ready. I'm glad I could solve that one problem, at least."

I gave her another hug and then settled the box onto the scarf. It looked perfect nestled there. I considered the foil-wrapped delicacy in my other hand and decided against leaving that there. When I looked at Lea, it was like she'd read my mind.

"I agree. Between the cats and the hobgoblin, that wouldn't make it through the day."

"We'll slice it up and serve it at the party," I said,

loving the idea. Then I had a thought. "You, um, didn't put anything extra in this, did you?"

Lea's eyes sparkled. "Maybe."

"There will be humans here."

"It's okay. It won't hurt them. Think of it as catnip for people."

I laughed. "As long as it doesn't make them climb the drapes."

A box of pretty red and green glass bulbs appeared in front of my face. Sebille's not-so-subtle reminder that we had a tree to decorate.

"What do you want me to do?" Lea asked, tugging off her coat.

"Can you get the big table from the back, find the tablecloth for it, and start arranging the food?"

She nodded briskly and took off toward the artifact library. I turned to the tree with my load of bulbs. With a slightly fizzy stomach that told me I was still worried about the evening to come, I set to work placing ornaments on the tree. Smiling and singing along with the music throbbing through the room with the force of a full orchestra, I felt my holiday spirit start to rise.

2

ALL WILL BE WELL. NOBODY WILL BE KILLED

"The snow outside is frightful, but the fire is sooooo delightful," Sebille screeched along with the magical orchestra in the box.

In his tank, Slimy tried unsuccessfully to drown himself in his little pond to escape her shrieking. I was glad I'd kept the water level low. Just in case.

In response to her caterwauling, Hex and Wicked ran growling from the room, the hair at the base of their tails standing straight up.

I let the sound float past me like white noise, happy for the orchestra to dull the full power of her shrieking. After checking the food one last time, I glanced up to the frog-shaped clock. Six-fifty-five. The guests should start arriving soon. Although, with the winter storm raging outside, I wasn't sure how many of them would brave it.

I ran sweaty palms down my black slacks and

took a deep breath, launching into the mantra I'd been reciting since Lea left and I'd gone upstairs to get ready for the shindig. Sebille had gone to her hidey hole in the artifact library, a location I still hadn't found, though not for lack of trying. The Sprite was being tricky. I suspected she'd been shifting locations to keep me on my toes.

It's going to be fine. The party will be fun. All will be well. Nobody will be killed.

I repeated the second half of the mantra several times. Just in case.

Movement on the sidewalk outside the big window told me somebody had arrived.

I hadn't been expecting the man who came through the door bearing a nicely wrapped gift. Standing near the food table, I kept my expression neutral. If I didn't keep my emotions firmly in check, my evening would start off very badly.

Grym gave me a tentative smile. "Hello, Naida."

I swallowed hard, my mouth filled with cotton. "Grym." I'd recently learned Detective Grym, a man I'd begun to think of as a friend, and maybe even a bit more, had ratted me out to the Société of Dire Magic. Not once, but several times. He'd almost cost me my job as Keeper of the Artifacts. Though he'd technically been correct in reporting my mistakes... since it was part of his job...it still burned me that he hadn't found a way around it.

Grym held up the gift. "I just wanted to bring

you this." When I made no move to take the package, Grym pointed toward the tree. "I'll just put it under the tree?"

I nodded, my heart beating hard enough to cause actual pain.

Grym stood in front of the tree for a moment, his handsome face filled with awe. "This is spectacular."

My gaze slid to Sebille's handiwork and, despite myself, I smiled. The tree looked like it was real. It smelled real. And the bulbs on its vibrant branches glowed with an almost ethereal illumination. The light caressed each ornament lovingly, highlighting its best features and giving it a soft glow.

Above the tree, falling seemingly from the ceiling above, a soft blanket of sparkling snowflakes drifted over the tree, creating a virtual snowfall to match the real snow beyond the windows. Lea's scarf was the perfect skirt, giving the tree a homey, yet elegant feel that I couldn't have created in a million years with a real tree skirt.

"Sebille and I had fun with it."

He nodded, settling the package onto the scarf next to Hobs' gift of Christmas spirit. "The music is beautiful."

"Yes," I said, simply, unsure how to find my way across the giant gulf between us.

He moved toward me, his big hands held out in front of him as if he wanted to take mine.

I jammed my hands into the pockets of my pants

to remove that temptation for both of us. I wasn't sure how I would feel about his touching me in that moment.

He stopped, dropping his hands to his sides. "I can't tell you how sorry I am, Naida."

I stared at him for a moment and then nodded. "I know."

"Will you ever forgive me?"

I honestly wasn't sure. "I don't know."

He sighed. "Okay. Well. I won't stay and ruin your party. I just wanted to stop by and give you that."

I don't know if he expected me to stop him from leaving. I'm not sure myself if I would have. The door opened on the moment with a merry jingle and Mrs. Foxladle bustled in, followed by Claudette Baxter, one of her book club friends, and Mr. Peabody, whose cheeks were pink from the cold.

They all wore happy smiles. When Mrs. Foxladle spotted Grym, she squealed in delight, enfolding him in a hug. She launched into an explanation to her friends about how the detective enjoyed the same book series she did and began to pester him again about joining the book club.

He didn't fight her very hard. I actually thought he might have joined, except that the club had begun holding their weekly meetings at Croakies. And Grym no longer knew whether he was welcome at my bookstore.

I greeted the ladies and Mr. Peabody, taking their coats with a promise to hang them up.

"I brought some goodies," Mrs. Foxladle said, indicating the small tin in her hand. "I'll just go put them on the table."

I thanked her and went to hang up the coats. Claudette Baxter squealed in delight, pointing toward the top of the nearest bookshelves. I followed her line of sight and felt all the blood leave my face.

Dressed in a tiny elf suit, with his red and white scarf wrapped around his neck, Hobs was perched on top of the shelf, a rosy glow in his cheeks and a sparkle in his blue eyes. He wore a pointed cap between his oversized ears and was kicking his heels against the books on the top shelf as he waved at the human partygoers.

My gaze flew to Grym. He gave me wide eyes.

The door between the library and the bookstore slammed open, and Sebille came running through, her eyes wild.

I caught her gaze and pointed to the top of the shelf.

She went pale, her freckles standing out like mud spots on her cheeks.

"Is it mechanical?" Mrs. Foxladle asked, a happy smile on her face.

"It's very lifelike, isn't it?" Mr. Peabody asked, chuckling.

I gave Sebille wide eyes and she nodded.

"We have lots of delicious food over here," I told the group. "Would everybody like some eggnog? Or maybe a cup of tea?"

I ushered them toward the food table as Sebille ran toward the shelves, gesturing wildly at Hobs.

With a delighted cackle, the little hobgoblin shot off the shelf and disappeared into the library, leaving a cartoon-like speed trail in his path, along with the dregs of his naughty cackle.

Sebille closed the door behind him and waved a hand over the knob, a suspicious green glow telling me she'd magically locked it against the little prankster.

"Wherever did you get it?" Claudette Baxter asked me. "He's so adorable. I'd love to get one for my kids."

I glanced toward the spot where Hobs had been and saw a blank-eyed replacement. Not quite as cute as the real thing, but much safer by far. I mouthed, "Thank you," to Sebille. She patted her chest to indicate that the hobgoblin had scared her near to death.

The bell on the front door jangled again and another group of party guests came inside, stomping snow off their boots and shivering dramatically. Lea came in on the tail end of the group, looking beautiful in a shimmery green sweater and black velvet skirt with tall leather boots. She'd pulled her long, light brown hair back into an intricate knot of braids and pinned a tiny red bow at the crown of her head.

She looked around, her turquoise eyes sparkling. "It looks beautiful, Naida." She clasped my hands and gave them a squeeze. "Lowering the lights was an inspired idea."

I greeted each of the new partygoers and sent them toward the food table.

"How can I help," Lea asked.

"Make sure people mingle?"

"I can do that." Lea headed toward the food, a wide smile on her pretty face. I thanked the goddess that she was my friend. Lea was a natural people-er, where I was less comfortable interacting on a personal level. People seemed to like her too, which made it a perfect situation.

The bell jangled again, a frosty blast of air blew another couple into the shop, the man having to duck quite a bit to keep from clocking his head on the door. I grinned when I saw who it was. "Theo!" Running over to embrace the giant, I felt like a three-year-old hugging her father. Even in his human-appropriate form, Theo was close to seven feet tall and probably weighed five to six hundred pounds. I turned to give his girlfriend, Birte, a hug. As always, she looked small standing next to Theo but was really of average height like I was. Birte was a beautiful silver dragon in her magic form, but as a human she was less attractive, with a muscular frame, sun-reddened skin that looked like she'd spent too much time outside, nervous pale-blue eyes, and wavy brown hair.

The pair were an odd match, but also proof that everybody could find love. Even a giant and a dragon.

"You look beautiful," I told Birte. She flushed, the color heightening her already ruddy completion. Her blue eyes sparkled with pleasure as she ran her hands over the silky black blouse she'd tucked into a pair of black jeans. "Thank you. Are the shoes too much?" I glanced down at the bright red pumps on her small feet.

"They're perfect!" I told her, giving her an impulsive hug. "Very festive."

Theo beamed at me when I glanced back his way. He held out an enormous hand to give me a wrapped gift. "For you."

Horror swamped me. I hadn't gotten him a gift. "Oh, Theo, you shouldn't have."

He inclined his head. "It was my pleasure."

"But I didn't get gifts..."

"He doesn't want anything in return, Naida," Birte said with an adoring look up at Theo. "He just likes to give." Her fingers touched a beautiful silver and diamond dragon hanging in the vee of her neckline.

"Birte, it's gorgeous!" I meant it too. The dragon

was every bit as elegant as she was in her natural form.

"Thank you. I love it." She looked down at her hands, seeming to realize she was holding a Holiday-decorated tin. "Oh, Theo made these. For the party."

A happy rumble sounded in Theo's throat. "Frosted Kabittle cookies. It's an ancient Gigantu family recipe."

"I'll just put these on the table," I told him. "Why don't you go say hi to Sebille."

To my everlasting shock, I noticed my assistant was holding court over by the tea counter. I assumed she was brewing tea for the gathering of regular customers there. I took a moment to enjoy Sebille's outfit for the night. In honor of the holidays, her usual knee-hi stockings were red, white, and green striped. She wore a bright green dress with a wide, shiny red belt that matched her red, Wicked Witch of the West shoes. With her pointed ears, red hair and luminous green eyes, she looked like a perfect Christmas Elf.

Grym stood apart from the others a bit. He didn't have a plate and was staring down at Mr. Slimy, whose glass tank was decorated with a drape of holly, complete with red berries. Sebille's idea.

"You should get some food," I told him, stopping beside the tank to catch his eye.

He glanced up, his face sad. "I will. In a minute."

I nodded, not sure what else to say. After a moment of silence, I started to move away.

Grym stopped me with a gentle hand on my wrist. "How's Rustin?"

I shrugged. "I'm not sure. I haven't heard from him since the whole Margot thing."

We'd all fought side by side a few weeks earlier to vanquish our mutual enemy Margot Quilleran, and the event had been a turning point for my friend, the ghost witch. Not in a good way.

I looked down at Mr. Slimy, whose blank, black gaze was watching me with more intensity than one would expect from a frog. "Mr. Slimy hasn't spoken to me since that night either." The frog had been infused with magic when Rustin had been sent into its body by his evil uncle and had begun to speak after a while. I missed his interminable questions and slightly snotty advice.

Grym's face turned more...well...grim. "That's not good."

I agreed but didn't want to think about it too much, for fear it would depress me. A hostess should definitely strive not to be depressed at her own party.

"Madeline will find a way to help them," Grym said. His hand slid from my wrist and clasped mine for a beat, giving it a squeeze before letting go.

I nodded, praying he was right.

"I'll just go get some *tea*," he said on a grin.

I laughed, knowing Sebille would slip a little something extra into Grym's tea. I hoped it warmed him up enough to enjoy himself a bit. I was mad at him, but that didn't mean I wanted him to be unhappy.

Much.

A soft clanging sound in my ear stopped me as I started toward my guests. I waited a bit, and it didn't sound again, so I forgot it.

I was saying goodbye to some early departing human guests who were worried about getting home in the snow when the clanging sounded again. I looked at Sebille. She pointed toward the connecting door.

Ah. Someone was trying to contact me through the communication mirror in the artifact library. Sebille had told me she'd spelled the mirror so I'd know when her mother, Queen Sindra of the local Fae, was trying to reach me.

I hurried across the bookstore and ducked quickly through the door. Two absolutely silent forms flashed past, brushing against my ankles as I hurried forward. I stumbled sideways, the cats nearly knocking me on my posterior. "Hey, you two," I yelled at the cats. They ignored me, of course, disappearing around the end of the artifact stacks.

The mirror was pulsing green around the edges of a black cloaking cloth as I approached it. Ever since I'd had a close call with a doppelganger spirit at Samhain, I'd been a little leery of mirrors, spending a lot less time in front of them than I used to.

Which was why the communication mirror was draped.

I tugged the black cloth away and found Queen Sindra hovering on the air, her wings throbbing at a speed that told me she was agitated. The familiar lushness of Lea's greenhouse, which was the Fae's new home, spread out behind her.

"Oh, thank the goddess, Naida. I've been so worried. Is everything okay there?"

"Everything's fine," I told her. "Why wouldn't it be?"

"I felt a magic wave a while ago. A powerful one." She squinted at me. "You didn't feel it?"

"No, I... Hold on." I glanced around for the Book of Pages, finding it on Shakespeare's desk where I'd left it. I touched the front of the book and the leather warmed beneath my touch, rolling as the magic engaged.

The book flipped open, the pages turning only two times before they stopped. A faint outline formed on the page, it looked like the beginning of an artist's sketch, the detail pale and unfocused. I carried the book back to the mirror. "Something's forming on this page, but it's very faint. I can't tell what it is."

She nodded. "If you'd like, I can bring a few of my soldiers to the party."

I considered her offer. "I'd love to have you come, Sindra. As guests. You *did* get the invite, didn't you?"

She flushed slightly. "Yes. I'm sorry we couldn't make it. We're having our own Yule celebration tonight."

"I completely understand. Maybe you'd like to stop by later? As guests. Whatever this wave means, Sebille and I can handle it."

She didn't look convinced. "It felt dark, Naida. Oily. And the city is about to close down under a weather advisory. You'll be trapped there."

"We'll be fine. Grym's here too. And Theo and Birte. We have a lot of firepower in this building right now."

Her hand twisting slowed along with her wings. "That's good news. But my offer stands. If you need some fairy muscle." She grinned. It always surprised me when the queen sounded like her daughter, rather than the cultured, elegant creature she was. I couldn't help wondering if Sebille had gotten her earthy side from her mother, or if she was corrupting the queen with her own earthiness. "Merry Christmas, Queen Sindra."

"Happy Yule to you, child. Take care."

I hung the cloth back over the mirror as she disappeared from view.

3

NOT FIT FOR MAN NOR BEASTIE

*T*he bell jangled as I came back into the bookstore. Sebille was hurrying toward the door and I headed toward the food table. Mrs. Foxladle was in an earnest conversation with Grym about their favorite cozy mystery series. It made me smile. I'd never get used to the idea of the big, burly cop reading cozy mysteries.

I spoke to Claudette and Mr. Peabody for a few minutes, lamenting the lack of desire to hit the busy stores for Christmas shopping.

A peal of happy laughter drew my attention to the door, and my eyes went wide as Sebille hugged a young, dark-haired man with rosy cheeks and wide, hazel eyes.

The man handed Sebille a package, and she tore the wrapping off of it like a child on Christmas morning. She pulled out a new e-cigarette kit and realization set in. I was probably looking at Devard, the owner of the vapery across the street. I'd pictured him much older and a lot grumpier.

The woman standing next to Devard handed my assistant a tin. She was tall for a woman, probably around five-nine or five-ten, and had pulled her light brown, curly hair back into a queue at the back of her neck and fixed a black velvet bow over it. The black dress she wore fit her shapely form snugly, the sleeves long enough to flare over her hands.

Sebille thanked her for the tin of goodies and hurried over to set it on the table. I was surprised when the three of them dropped into chairs by the window and fell into a pleasant conversation that might have revolved around vaping since they all broke out their e-cigs and proceeded to puff away.

I'd thought Sebille and Devard were on the outs, ever since he'd evicted Sebille from her tiny apartment above the vapery for turning one of Devard's customers into a slug in the midst of a vaped fog.

Now, before you say, but vaping doesn't alter the mind, you must realize you haven't tried one of Sebille's "special" vape mixtures.

I had a sudden horrified thought and started toward them, worried that Sebille might break out some of her special brew at the party.

The last thing I needed was for her to turn Mr. Peabody into a slimy critter from the terrestrial gastropod mollusk family.

They looked up as I approached. Devard stood, smiling widely. He held out a hand as I reached him. "You must be Naida. I'm Devard Othco. It's a pleasure to finally meet you. I'm sorry I haven't made it over here to introduce myself."

I shook his hand, returning his smile. "The pleasure's mine."

He nodded. "Thank you for inviting me to the party."

I barely kept from skimming Sebille a glance. I hadn't invited Devard since the last I'd heard he and Sebille were on the outs. Which meant Sebille had invited him. "I'm so glad you could come."

"Have you met Rhonda?" Sebille asked.

Rhonda clutched an e-cig between long, perfectly manicured nails, which I noticed were bright red with tiny white Christmas trees on them. The woman gave me a crooked smile. "Hey, Naida."

I offered her my hand. "It's nice to meet you." I didn't remember inviting a Rhonda to the party. "How do you and Sebille know each other?"

"She lives in the building next to mine," Devard said. "She comes into the vapery a lot."

"Ahh," I nodded. *I'd bet my favorite boots, Rhonda was the Banshee Sebille always complained about because of her screaming.* "I'm really glad you could make it."

Devard nodded toward the last three remaining non-magic guests. "There are humans here?"

I nodded, pleased by the opening he'd given me. "Mrs. Foxladle, Claudette, and Mr. Peabody are some of my best customers. If you could keep the magic vaping down until they leave, I'd greatly appreciate it."

Devard slid Sebille a glance, his grin widening. "You heard the woman, Sebille. No turning anyone into slugs."

My cranky assistant giggled. She. Actually. Giggled. I swallowed hard, remembering Sindra's warning. Was the dark magic infecting Sebille?

"You have to try one of these," Lea said from behind me.

I turned to find a frosted sugar cookie under my nose. The delightful scent of sugar and vanilla drifted into my sinuses and lured me like a siren's song. I took the cookie and bit into it, my eyes going closed in pure bliss. "Oh, that's amazing. Who brought these?"

Lea shrugged, polishing off her own cookie. "I don't know, but whoever it was, they're magical. Theo's had about ten of them, but the supply just keeps replenishing."

I excused myself and surreptitiously dropped the cookie into the trash behind the sales counter. I couldn't afford to fall under the magical influence of sugar and butter. I needed to keep my wits about me so I could watch for potential problems at the party. Having my human *and* magical acquaintances together in one place was a bit nerve-making. I was confident that my magical guests had lived among humans long enough to be aware of the pitfalls and savvy enough to avoid them, but there was always the Hobs side of the equation, which gave me plenty to worry about.

I glanced toward the dividing door, seeing the faint green glow on the knob that told me it was still painted with Sebille's magical lock.

Good. That should keep Hobs out of the bookstore.

I relaxed slightly.

"Who's that guy?" a deep voice asked.

I looked up to find Grym shoving a bite of cookie into his mouth. He held a second cookie in his other hand.

"Those are good, aren't they?"

He made a delirious face that turned my belly warm. "Incredible. I need to find out who brought them. I want the recipe."

The enticing scent of sugar and vanilla wafted through the air and my fingers twitched toward the cookie he was still holding. I fisted my hand and fought the impulse to steal it. "If I had to guess, I'd say it was Mrs. Foxladle. She's an amazing cook."

He shook his head. "I've asked everybody."

"Not even Theo? He brought cookies."

"Theo's mouth hasn't been empty enough to talk in ten minutes."

I laughed. "Well, giants do love their sugar."

Rhonda walked past us and smiled, disappearing into the bathroom.

Grym nodded toward Devard. "Who's the guy with Sebille?"

"That's her friend from across the street. Devard owns the vapery where she used to have an apartment."

"The guy who kicked her out?"

I nodded, frowning slightly.

"They look pretty chummy."

"Yes, they do, don't they?"

"Have you seen my hair bow?" Lea asked me, reaching up to feel around in the spot where the velvet hair decoration had been.

"No. It's probably somewhere near those cookies," I teased her. "You've been spending all your time there."

"Ha," she said, narrowing her eyes at me.

The bell jangled as the front door opened, letting a blustery slice of winter inside to dust the carpet with snow. A very small couple with red noses and bead-like black eyes that were barely visible under a matching pair of red knitted hats stumbled in, shivering violently. I'd never seen the couple before, but they seemed to be in some distress.

Grym and I hurried over. "Are you okay?"

The man draped an arm around his wife, tugging her close as she shivered so hard her teeth clanked together. "Our car slid off the road a couple of miles from here. We've been trying to find a place to call for help. This is the first place we saw that was open."

I pointed toward the round table near the bookshelves. "Come in. Sit down. Let me get you something hot to drink. We have hot chocolate, tea or coffee."

"Hot chocolate, please," the woman said in a soft, quivery voice.

"I'll get it," Sebille said, hurrying past.

"Thanks, Sebille." I reached for my phone, finding it useless.

"Cell service is out," Devard said from inches away.

I turned in surprise to find him right behind me.

He held up his phone. "I just tried to call over to the vapery to make sure they closed up and got out of there. The storm is building fast. It's supposed to be a bad one."

I worried my bottom lip with my teeth, wondering if I should send everyone home.

As if he'd read my mind, Grym said. "It's probably safer for them here."

"He's right," the man sitting at the table said. "It's deadly out there. Visibility is horrible and the wind is brutal. The snow feels like tiny icicles falling from the sky."

Bat's boogers! I fought not to show my panic at his

words. The last thing I was prepared for was an all-night sleepover party for a dozen of my most magically diverse...or averse...friends.

Sebille put two steaming mugs of hot chocolate in front of them. The delicious scent of rich chocolate filled the air, and I noted the tiny marshmallows floating across the surface of the decadent chocolate with a smile.

"Thank you so much," the woman breathed, holding her mug in two hands and sipping it with obvious pleasure. "That tastes wonderful."

"Would you like some food?" I asked. "We have lots."

They shook their heads. "No, but thank you," the man said. "This is perfect for now. Please, don't let us keep you from your party."

"It's fine," I told them. "You're my guests too." I gave them a smile that I hoped was welcoming. They seemed to relax.

Grym sat down at the table with them. "Where were you heading before you slid off the road?"

The couple shared a look and the woman pulled her coat open, revealing a typical Elf's costume, based on corny human mythology. "We're supposed to be elves at the mall." She grimaced. "It's probably a madhouse there."

The man chuckled. "I don't suppose they'll invite us to do it again after we're no shows."

His wife nodded. "I'm having trouble working up a negative reaction to that thought at the moment."

We all chuckled.

An orchestral strain of *A Fairy in the Christmas Tree* began playing, the rich sound saturating the room with emotion. The man closed his eyes. "Gorgeous." His eyes flew open. "You have a Soul of Christmas box. Where'd you get it?"

Grym and I shared a look. "Umm," I said.

The woman lifted the knitted cap off her ears, showing me the points. "It's okay. You're the Keeper, aren't you?"

Human hybrid Elves. Not Fae. Not really. But they were born with a tiny bit of magic, mostly of the cloaking variety, and lived their lives looking like the human version of Santa's little helpers. Some of them resisted the humiliating stereotype and tried to mask their most telling features, but some, like my Elvin guests apparently, decided not to fight fate and found jobs in film and theater playing the creatures they resembled.

Before I responded, I glanced toward the three humans near the food, seeing them happily occupied and not paying attention to us. Then I nodded. "A friend of mine gave it to me for Christmas."

"Where is it?" the man demanded. "I need to see it."

I didn't like the way he asked, so I ignored the

question. "How long have you been playing Santa's helpers at the mall?"

The woman chuckled. "I believe this will be our fifth year, isn't that right Eattle?"

"That sounds right, Earline."

The strange names nearly made me smile. "Well, I guess I'll go mingle. Please make yourselves at home."

A plaintive yowl sounded on the other side of the dividing door. I veered in that direction just as Mr. Peabody came out of the small bathroom and nearly ran into me.

"Oh, hello, Naida. I'm sorry." He wavered a bit on his feet, his eyes going momentarily crossed.

"Are you all right?" I asked him, reaching out to touch his arm in case he started to fall.

"I'm fine. I think I just had too much of Sebille's special tea." He winked at me, and I slid my assistant a look. She was standing by the window, waving her arms expansively as she spoke to Devard.

"Maybe you should stick to the eggnog for a while," I told the elderly man. "And have some food."

He nodded and tottered toward the food table.

I hurried over to Sebille. "Can I talk to you for a minute?"

She turned a bright smile on me, her eyes looking a bit glassy. "What's up, boss?"

The music came to a crescendo and dropped to a

dramatic pause, which was filled by dual yowling on the other side of the dividing door.

I glanced that way, torn.

"You should let the furry rats in, Naida," Sebille slurred.

I glared at her. "I need to speak to you for a moment." I turned to Devard. "If you'll excuse us for a moment...?"

He nodded and I tugged Sebille toward the center aisle of the bookshelves. I stopped in my tracks when I saw Mrs. Foxladle sitting in one of the reader chairs at the center, her gaze following something only she could see and her hands reaching to bat it away.

I turned to Sebille. "Did you spike everybody's tea?" I asked in a harsh whisper.

She reared back, nearly toppling over and having to take a couple of steps to keep from falling. Placing a hand dramatically on her chest, she fixed her face into a shocked expression. "Moi?"

"Yes, Vous!" I said, well past the last shred of my patience. "You've made everybody drunk." A sudden thought made me yelp in horror. I ran to the front of the store again and looked at the two Elves. They were still sitting at the table, still sipping their hot chocolate and seemed to be fine. They'd removed their hats and coats and were chatting with Claudette Baxter.

My heart rate dropped to a reasonable level.

Apparently, my irresponsible assistant hadn't drugged Eattle and Earline's cocoa. That was something, at least. The last thing I needed was a lawsuit from two complete strangers being drugged against their will.

Somebody tugged a curly strand of my dark brown hair. I turned with a glower to find Sebille wavering before me. "I din...didn...didn't spike anything."

She was clearly under the influence of something. And I wasn't sure I could trust anything she had to say. But something passed through her iridescent green gaze. Something wary and touched with fear. And I realized she was telling me the truth. "If not you, then who?"

She wobbled there for a moment, and then her eyes went wide. We both said his name at the same time.

"Hobs!"

I turned on my heel, heading for the artifact library.

"Wait, Naida!" Sebille called out. She started to fall sideways and caught herself on the shelves. "What d...do...doooo...doooyou want me ta do?"

I wrenched the door open and two sleek gray forms shot into the room, tails whipping angrily. "Make coffee. Lots of it. And see if Lea can do something."

Sebille gave me a jaunty salute that sent her

reeling sideways. She stumbled into the aisle between the shelves and I had no idea if she hit the ground or not. I let the connecting door slam shut behind me and went in search of the naughty hobgoblin.

4

IT AIN'T FOR THE BLEEPS AND FRAIDYS

"*H*obs!"

Silence met my shout, deep and almost pulsing with expectation. It was much quieter than it should have been.

"Hobs, come here, please."

Nothing.

I closed my eyes and engaged my keeper magic, tuning into the artifact library at a detailed level, so that I felt the pulse of everything inside the massive space. I sensed a tension running through the room, a slight thrum in the magic that told me something wasn't quite right.

But no Hobs.

Where was he? "Hobs! You're scaring me. Come out here right now."

High above my head, something shifted. I looked

up to find SB staring down at me. "What be twisting yer mainsail, Lass?"

"Have you seen Hobs?"

SB lifted his wings and floated down to me, landing on my shoulder amid a storm of downy under-feathers. "Walked the blackguard off the plank, meself, not a quarter-hour past."

Since we had no plank, or large body of water to float it over, I wasn't overly concerned by his statement. I chose to glom onto the part that told me Hobs had been there. "You saw him? Which way did he go?"

SB danced sideways, lifting his wings, the ratty feathers scraping along my cheek. "Down, down, down to the belly of the sea. The lad sank like a bloody rock, and at the bottom he be."

I rolled my eyes. "SB, I don't have time for your limericks. This is important."

"Bwawk!" He rose in alarm as the dividing door flew open, crashing against the wall behind it. I spun to face the person standing in the doorway, the small, rotund form encased in a red velvet jacket with fake fur trim and green and red striped socks, which ended in jaunty green slippers that curved upward at the toes.

Earline's rosy round face was fixed in an expression of awe, her black eyes filled with the same emotion.

How in the goddess's best lace panties had the

Elf opened that door? It still had Sebille's magical lock on it. "Earline. Can I help you find something?"

The black button eyes roved around the library, widening as they took in the massive array of magical artifacts. "Oh, my!" she murmured.

I hurried forward, blocking the artifact library with my body as I gently pushed her back into the bookstore. A messy collection of red and green feathers whirled past my ear, and SB flew squawking into the bookstore.

My guests all turned to exclaim in surprise as the parrot made a circuit above their heads. "Drink yer ration o' grog, ye lads, sup yer thimble miladies. It's a bloody cold night that'll freeze yer bleeps, and it ain't for the bleeps and fraidys."

Claudette Baxter squealed happily, clapping her hands as SB swooped past and made a lewd suggestion above her head.

I closed my eyes, striving for calm. Then opened them again as an icy hand touched my skin.

Earline, looking concerned.

"Are you okay, Naida keeper?"

I nodded, forcing a smile. "I'm fine. Were you looking for something?"

Earline frowned. "Yes. I can't find Eattle. I checked the stacks of books. By the way, there's an elderly lady in there who seems to be rather inebriated." She frowned with disapproval. "Hopefully, you're not serving spirits here?"

I shook my head. "I'm not, no. She's probably just tired." It was a lame excuse. I felt guilty for implying that Mrs. Foxladle might be suffering from night dementia, but it was all that came to mind. "I'll check on her."

Something brushed against my leg and whirled away before I could identify it. Hex or Mr. Wicked, no doubt, enjoying the party and all the food they were finding on the floor. I firmly closed the dividing door, checking to make sure it still glowed green. Just in case, I sent a wisp of keeper magic into it to reinforce Sebille's lock. Earline should not have been able to open that door.

Unless I'd left it slightly ajar by mistake.

Deciding that had probably been what happened, I pushed that bit of worry aside. "He wouldn't be back there. You checked the bathroom?" I glanced toward the small bathroom. The door was open. It was empty. "Maybe he stepped outside for some air?"

Earline sent a worried gaze toward the big window behind the tree. The snow was coming down in thick sheets, blocking out everything except the faint, eerie glow of the street light behind it. "I hope not. Maybe we should send out a search party for him."

I barely bit back a grimace. The last thing I wanted to do was send my guests out into the storm. "I could probably scrape up a couple of people to help with that." I patted her arm. "Let me see what I can do."

I approached Grym first. He was standing near the window, looking out into the snow.

"Did you see Eattle leave through this door?"

Grym looked surprised. "No. He'd have to be crazy to have gone out in this. You can't see three feet in front of you out there."

I stared into the falling snow, worry burrowing through my stomach. "Earline thinks he went outside. She wants us to go search for him."

Grym slid the small, round woman a look. "Did she check the bathroom?"

"It's empty." I let him see the concern on my face. "She opened the door into the artifact library."

"Did you forget to lock it?"

I bit back irritation. In his shoes, I'd have probably asked the same question. "Double locked. Sebille reinforced it."

His expression turned even more serious. "I don't like this."

A woman stumbled past, bumping into me and turning with a smile to apologize. "Naida, I'm so sorry. I guess I'm a little light-headed from the vape I just tried. Sebille offered me a very unique mixture." It was Claudette Baxter, her cheeks rosy and her cloud of blonde hair slightly askew as if she'd repeatedly run her fingers through it.

I hadn't known Claudette vaped, but I seemed to

remember she used to be a smoker so it wasn't really that unusual for her to have taken up vaping.

Her words struck horror in my heart. "Sebille broke out her special vapes?"

Claudette's smile was wide, slightly crooked. "I know, exciting, huh." She glanced around, frowning. "Have you seen my purse?"

"What does it look like?" I asked.

"Tiny and black, about yay big." She held her hands about five inches apart. "It has a long silver chain on it."

"No, sorry. I haven't seen it. But I'll keep my eyes open."

Frowning, she nodded. "Thanks. Maybe I left it over by the food table. Everything tastes so delicious. Especially those cookies."

I looked at Grym, and he shook his head. "You're going to have to start a 'lost and found' after tonight."

"What do you mean?"

"I've lost my keys. I was going to leave earlier, but I couldn't find them anywhere."

"You don't have to leave, Grym. It's okay."

"Well, as it turns out, I can't anyway. The roads are impassable now."

A plate of food appeared in front of me. I turned to find Lea, her turquoise gaze slightly twitchy. "I brought you some food. You haven't had a minute to visit and eat."

"I'm not really hungry."

"Eat!" she ordered, then giggled. "Sorry. I channeled my mother there for a minute."

"I'm really not…"

She picked up a cookie and stuffed it into my mouth. There was nothing I could do but take a bite. I chewed and swallowed, dropping the cookie back onto the plate. "There, are you happy now?"

"Nope. Two more bites of cookie and then you can eat your vegetables." She giggled again, wheeling away to join the other guests, whom I was just noticing, seemed to be equally giddy.

"This is the drunkest party I've ever been to where nobody's drinking."

Grym took a cookie from the plate and held it up. "Maybe it's these cookies. Have you noticed the smell of them follows you all around the room?"

I inhaled deeply, enjoying the scent of sugar and vanilla. "It smells like Christmas."

Grym took a huge bite, swallowing and eyeing my plate. "Are you going to eat that?"

I handed him the plate. "Help yourself. Do you think we should go out looking for Eattle?"

Grym shook his head. "He's probably under the table or behind the stacks. If he'd gone out this door, I would have seen him."

My gaze slid to Earline and worry niggled. The woman stood all by herself, her hands crossed in front of her. She seemed to be guarding the connecting door as if she believed Eattle was in there.

I scanned my mind back over my quick visit there, trying to remember if the Elf could have slipped through. I was almost certain I'd pulled the door snugly closed. He'd have had to be invisible and really fast to get through behind me.

Though, Earline had gotten the door open. Seemingly without even trying.

The bites of cookie in my stomach turned sour.

A heavy drumbeat preceded a booming rendition of the little drummer boy, coming from the Soul of Christmas box. Each beat was like an extra heartbeat in my chest. The powerful concussive sound was like a shot of adrenaline to my system, ratcheting up my stress level until it felt as if my heart was in my throat.

A wave of dizziness made me wobble on my feet. I took a deep breath and braced myself against the shelves.

"Naida, did you take the tea strainer? I wanna make..." Sebille's voice trailed off and she cocked her head, her gaze sliding upward, to something I couldn't see. "Pretty."

Had everyone but me lost their minds...?

A large butterfly, iridescent green and purple like a Sprite's wings, fluttered past. I squinted at it, trying to figure out how a butterfly had gotten into Croakies in the dead of winter. "Where did you come from, pretty one?" I stuck a finger out and the butterfly landed on it, waving its antenna at me and smiling widely. "Hello," I said. "What's your name?"

"Naida?" someone said.

"I'm Bob."

Well, that didn't seem right. "Bob? Really?"

"Yes. Bob. With two Os."

I thought about that for a minute and then giggled. "You're lying."

"Naida!" A big hand clawed my shoulder and shook me so hard poor Boob went flying off into the distance. I reached for him, crying out his name. "No, wait, Boob!"

"Naida! Pull yourself together."

I focused on the hand on my shoulder. It was *really* big. My gaze followed the arm to the shoulder, then to the face owned by the hand and I jumped, giving a squeal of alarm.

It was a giantnormous face. "Wow, you're big."

Theo narrowed his eyes at me. "Naida, you were talking to the air and screaming boob."

I giggled again. "Boob had iridescent green and purple wings."

Mrs. Foxladle stumbled up. She held Boob on her finger.

"You found Boob!" I exclaimed.

Mrs. Foxladle giggled. "I did. Such a nice butterfly."

Theo shook his head. "Naida keeper, I wanted to

tell you that Birte and I aren't feeling well. We're going home."

I nodded, patting him clumsily on the shoulder. "Be careful. It's snowing hard out there."

Theo nodded. "Merry Christmas, Naida."

"Happy Yule, Theo."

I waved at Birte and almost fell over. Another wave of dizziness turned the world into a merry-go-round.

I wanted to get off.

"I don't feel so good," Mrs. Foxladle said. I wrapped an arm around her. "Let's sit down," I suggested, guiding her to a chair. "I'll go get us some water."

She nodded, rubbing circles on her temples with her fingertips.

I started toward the small refrigerator in the tea area. I didn't get far.

The music of the Soul of Christmas box suddenly stopped. The silence was violent in its abruptness. I jolted to a stop.

All movement halted around me and conversation died.

We were like figures in a video when somebody hits the *Pause* button.

The lack of sound made the air feel spongy and the floor beneath my feet seemed to quiver, nearly tossing me to the ground in my dizzy state. I grabbed hold of Slimy's tank, looking down into his fathomless black gaze.

"Ribbit?" His froggy question was startling in the pure, unwavering silence.

"I don't know..." I managed to respond. My voice echoed through my mind and bled out my ears to fall to the ground.

All the lights went out. Even the street lamp outside was doused.

The room was completely, unrelentingly dark.

The floor shook again. The air compressed against me until I felt my bones start to crunch together. The sensation was brutal, violent, and wrung a pain-filled scream from my throat.

The floor dropped out from under me and I started to fall, clawing helplessly at the air as I plummeted into the deep, velvety blackness, helpless to do anything but wait for the end of the void.

Someone else screamed, the sound raw, broken, and feral.

I never hit bottom. But after a moment, I did stop. I moved my legs, trying to figure out where I was, and my foot splashed into water.

The water felt strange against my skin. Almost like I was insulated against it.

The lights suddenly flashed on and we all stood there, blinking.

A panel of smeared glass separated me from the rest of the room. Everybody looked funny...slightly skewed, like I was looking at them through a magnifying glass, and colors were off.

I blinked and something snapped beneath my gaze. I looked down and saw...

I saw...

Oh, my goddess, I saw squatty green legs and funny looking webbed feet.

Ribbit!

A long, sticky tongue snapped out of my mouth, snatching a forgotten cricket leg off a nearby rock.

My stomach roiled. Had I just eaten a bug?

Ribbit!

My yelp of disgust came out sounding like Mr. Slimy.

I screamed.

Ribbit! Ribbit! Ribbit! Ribbit! Ribbit!

5

SQUISHY GREEN HEART ATTACK

A few beats later, I forced myself to stop ribbiting. My little green heart still beat hard in my squishy green chest, but I shoved terror down and looked around the room.

SB was doing barrel rolls across the Croakies airspace, his beak open in a constant shriek and feathers raining down on everyone.

A full-blown Gargoyle stood in the center of the room, staring down at his boulder-like hands in wonder. He had a bright red feather balanced on one rocky shoulder.

Mrs. Foxladle was looking at her hands like she'd never seen them before.

Mr. Peabody stood a few feet away from Slimy's... my...tank, his faded gaze sliding to mine in question.

Air sifted past on the thrumming sound of massive wings, and my pulse picked up in remembered panic. My gaze jerked toward the ceiling, to the silver dragon perched atop the bookshelves, head hunched against its chest in the limited space. The dragon's wings were tiny in relation to its long, sleek body, but they were still huge and crunched atop the bookshelves they were in danger of ripping the tiles down on my old-fashioned tin and plaster ceiling.

The dragon looked dazed, its beautiful eyes slightly unfocused. That was a calamity waiting to happen.

I looked around for Theo, hoping he could help Birte rein in her magical form and return safely to her human shape.

He was nowhere to be found.

Panic threatened to jumpstart my nervous little green heart again. I was looking at a full-blown disaster with the potential to become cataclysmic. Obviously, somebody had released some kind of spell into the party. If I didn't do something fast, people were going to get hurt. And then there was the fact that my human friends were likely to drop dead of heart attacks when they fully comprehended that they were looking upon the creatures of mythology. Some of them no doubt terrifying to the unprepared mind.

I looked for Lea, finding her standing near the dividing door, her pretty turquoise gaze blank and blinking. She kept swallowing as if something was caught in her throat and, as I watched, her tongue shot out and swept the air in front of her.

Without warning, the Soul of Christmas music box started playing again. I glanced toward the tree, seeing the tiny box nestled in a fold of Lea's thick scarf. At least that was still safe and working. Maybe the music would soothe everyone and keep the potential carnage to a minimum.

A door slammed, dragging my gaze back to Lea. A strand of her light brown hair blew away from her face, and I realized the door I'd heard slamming had been the dividing door.

What the...?

The dragon's head jerked up and smashed into the ceiling, putting a nice dragonhead-sized dent in my pretty tiles.

"Ribbit!"

The dragon shook its head, roaring, and took a step, its enormous, clawed foot hitting only air as it stepped off the narrow bookshelf. The enormous creature teetered there for a beat and then dug its claws into the shelving, tearing huge chunks out of the highly polished wood.

"Ribbit!" I objected.

SB shot past the dragon, flying straight, if a little wobbly still, and the sleek, silver head shot up again in surprise, bashing another dent into my ceiling.

I sagged down into my fat, squishy body, depression making me limp. "Ribbit..." I sighed.

"Naida!"

I twitched at the sound of my name. My black gaze climbing upward. I jerked in surprise, hopping sideways and splashing into Slimy's little pond as SB landed on the edge of my tank.

"Naida, is that you?"

I'd never realized how terrifying the parrot was before. What if it decided to attack? I had zero defenses.

Unless I whacked it with my tongue.

Bird blisters!

Then I realized who was speaking to me. I jumped in excitement. "Lea?"

Lea SB tossed her colorful head. "Yeah, it's me. Thank the goddess I found you."

"How'd you know it was me?" I asked my friend.

"I saw you hopping around croaking at the dragon when it dented your ceiling." She laughed, but it came out as a squawk.

"What kind of spell is this?" I asked my friend.

"I'm not absolutely sure, but I think it's a 'You're me but who am I?' hex." She danced around the edge of the tank, lifting her wings. "We need to find Sebille."

"Why?" I asked.

"Because that's typically a Fae spell."

I had a horrible thought. "You don't think that Hobs...?"

The parrot's head cocked back and forth as if Lea

SB was trying to shake it in the negative. "It's unlikely. This goes well beyond mischief. There's real potential for deadly results here, Naida."

Gosling goobers!

As if the Universe was inspired by her suggestion, the dragon roared again and lifted its wings, taking another step and falling off the shelves. The enormous magical creature pounded its wings in a frantic tempo, but there wasn't enough room or time for it to catch air and it became a giant, silver missile headed right for me, Lea, and three other guests who stood nearby.

"Ribbit!" I screamed in warning, catching the attention of the Gargoyle, who'd gone from examining his hands to knocking on his knees like a physician testing for reflex reactions.

The Gargoyle straightened in a jolt and, seeing the dragon heading toward Mrs. Foxladle, threw himself into the air and snagged the panicked creature around the middle, landing in a crouch. He held the big creature above the ground in his rock-like arms, grunting with the effort. The impact of their landing shook my glass tank and liquid trickled to the ground beneath me.

Oops! Did I do that?

Rhonda ran toward the Gargoyle, ducking the dragon's flailing claws and wildly whipping wings. "Bring her in here!" the Banshee screamed, running toward the connecting door and wrenching it open.

"Buzzard belches!" I exclaimed in a voice only Lea SB could hear. "Can everybody open that door?"

The parrot hopped up and landed again in a spray of feathers. "Something hinky's been done to that lock."

"Ya think?" I croaked.

The Gargoyle took a step, groaning loudly with the effort of holding onto the writhing dragon, and barked out a yelp of pain as one of the creature's claws raked along his side.

The sound startled the dragon into another roar. The terrorized creature belched a thick ribbon of fire into the air, directly at Mrs. Foxladle.

"Ribbit! Ribbit! Ribbit!" I screamed in panic.

At the last second, the Gargoyle managed to wrench the dragon sideways, and the flames missed the elderly woman by mere inches, searing a trail down a row of magical texts instead.

"Ribbit! Ribbit! Ribbit!"

I really needed to pull myself together.

A head shot up from the central area of the bookshelves. It was a massive head. The size of a small car, massive. *Theo*! Shoulders the width of the center aisle rolled under the huge head, and the giant started to move. The building shuddered under his thunderous footsteps. Glass rattled in the window frames. Books fell from shelves and hit the floor with ominous ripping sounds.

Smoke filled the open space at the front of the

store. Theo pushed through like a terrible, mythical creature cutting through the fog on a Celtic battlefield. He lifted his head and his nostrils flared. It was clear he was in his most basic, most feral form and, depending on whether it was actually Theo at the wheel or one of the others who had no idea what it meant to be a giant in the human world, we were looking at possible total devastation.

Especially if the boyfriend part of Theo's brain took exception to the current manhandling of his girlfriend, the dragon.

Theo's eyes found the writhing dragon, who took that moment to release another thick ribbon of flame, barely missing the Gargoyle and threatening to roast a parrot for dinner, and he roared.

People screamed, running for cover as the threat of imminent crushing, maiming, and gastronomic disaster finally filtered through their magic-fogged brains.

I hopped into the air and landed with a splash.

Yeah, that was totally unsatisfying as a reaction. "Lea!" I screamed. "We have to do something fast."

"I can't spell without fingers, Naida," she squawked out.

Mr. Peabody ran over to the tank, looking down on me with panicked eyes. "Naida? Is that you?"

"Ribbit."

He glanced at the parrot. "Is this Naida?"

"Yes," Lea squawked in SB's voice. "And who might ye be, ye scallywag?"

Oh, no! Blackbeard's magic was infusing SB. We'd soon need a pirate gibberish translator to understand Lea SB.

"I'm Grym."

Grym! That was good. Or was it? In Mr. Peabody's body, he wasn't much use in corralling a giant or a dragon.

Near the dividing door, Rhonda was looking at her hands and scrunching her face as if she was trying to call magic but couldn't. I was pretty sure the only magic Banshees had was in their scream. They could immobilize whole masses of people with a single, mind-numbing scream.

That's it!

"Tell Rhonda to scream," I told Lea.

The parrot bounced its head in a movement I interpreted as agreement and took off, flying directly toward Rhonda.

Theo's hand shot out and fingers as long as one of my human arms grabbed for the parrot, probably intending to make itself some poached parrot for Christmas dinner. Fortunately, Lea SB was getting the hang of her wings and shot skyward, avoiding the clumsy grab.

The dragon shot fire at the parrot and Lea swung sideways...too fast...falling into a barrel-roll and smacking up against the top corner of a bookshelf.

I winced...well twitched...as I watched her slide to the ground and land in a heap.

Fortunately, Grym was a quick study. "Scream!" he yelled at the Banshee.

Rhonda stopped scrunching and straining, and her eyes lit up with understanding.

She stepped toward the dragon, tilted her head back, and opened her mouth.

And opened it.

And kept opening it.

Her jaw unhinged until her mouth was the size of a dinner plate, filled with razor-sharp teeth and an oversized, forked tongue.

Ew!

I'd read about Banshee screams. Their mouths were built to create a wide range of pitches, aided by a tongue which was shaped like a tuning fork, and several rows of teeth that focused the scream as it emerged.

But reading about their screams had done nothing to prepare me for one.

I suddenly realized that I needed to do something to keep from hearing the scream, or I'd be immobilized too.

"Ribbit! Ribbit! Ribbit!" I screamed at Grym. He frowned and then seemed to understand. He grabbed a teacup from the counter behind him and dropped it over my head.

Blades of sound sliced through the room.

Each fat, overstretched note undulated with unique power, lifting, diving, slicing deep. The scream built inside my head until it pulsed against my brain, puncturing holes in it like a thousand tiny needles. There was no pain. Not really. Only an unrelenting pressure that filled my skull until it felt like it would explode.

Then the sound changed. It dulled to a thunderous throb, pounding, pounding, pounding until I was sure it had turned my brain to mush.

My eardrums shrank away from the sound. Fluid ran from my nose. I prayed it wasn't blood.

In the blink of an eye, the throbbing eased into a low, rhythmic hum. My limbs softened. My mind numbed. And it was suddenly all I could do to blink. I tried to move one of my bent, green legs and it was like moving through quicksand.

But my leg *did* move.

And, a moment later, my teacup lifted, and I was looking up into Rhonda's angry face.

"Ribbit?" I asked.

Rhonda rolled her brown eyes. "Quit screwing around, Naida. Your party's a mess. We need to get rid of this spell and find out who's doing this and why."

Hello, Sebille.

6

USE YOUR WORDS...

*N*early everyone in the place was locked into inactivity, their open eyes unblinking, and their limbs frozen into the positions they'd been in before the scream.

I threw myself against the smeared glass a few times to let Sebille know I wanted out of the tank.

She rolled her eyes again. I hoped Rhonda's eyelids were ready for the workout they were about to receive. "Use your words, Naida."

"Get me out of here, you derk!"

"Tisk," she said, grinning. "Language."

"Buffalo boohind! I'll language *you*, Sprite. This party was all your idea. Now, look what's happened!"

"Calm down, Naida," said a gentle voice. I turned to give Grym Peabody a glare. "You zippit, Gargoyle. Why couldn't you have grabbed a body that could do magic?"

I knew I was flying completely off the chain, but I was at my wits end.

Lea SB landed heavily on the edge of the tank. I was surprised she'd been unaffected by the scream. "Avast ye maties. Arrr, what folly is this?" she asked.

I translated that to mean, "Why's everybody playing statue?"

"Banshee scream," Grym Peabody offered.

"Ah!" she said. "Genius."

"Thanks," Sebille Rhonda and I both said.

I gave my assistant a froggy glare for taking the credit.

"Why weren't you trapped by it?" I asked Lea.

"I was adrift in Davy Jones locker."

In other words, she'd knocked herself out when she hit the shelves. Good thing SB's body was already dead. I looked at Grym and Sebille translated my question for him.

He shrugged. "I plugged my ears and hid in the closet."

I turned my blank froggy gaze to Sebille. "I guess you don't have any magic to call in that form?"

Sebille Rhonda grimaced. "You've seen the extent of it."

We all looked at Lea SB.

Her feathers ruffled. "Arrr! What do ye propose I do with these?" She lifted a claw and almost toppled backward off the tank. Fluttering her wings, she managed to stay upright but she overcorrected and fell into the tank with me.

I really wished I could roll my eyes. I settled for whacking her on the beak with my tongue.

"Urgh! Reptilian blackguard! It's the plank for thee!"

Sebille gave Rhonda's eyelids another roll. "There's got to be another way to get rid of this hex."

I remembered what Lea had told me. "This is a Fae spell, right?"

Lea and Sebille nodded. "Then maybe your mother could reverse it," I told Sebille.

She shrugged. "Maybe, but how are we going to contact her?"

I hadn't considered that. In Rhonda's form, she couldn't work the communication mirror. I couldn't do it either. "Who has our real forms?"

I looked around but didn't see Sebille's green-and-red-clad person. Lea was still standing in front of the dividing door, though.

Make that crouching. She looked ready to spring, and her tongue was sticking straight out of her mouth as if she'd been caught in the midst of trying to snatch a fly from the air.

"You're Mr. Slimy," I said, my gaze sliding to the parrot.

"Gah!" SB said, with swashbuckler disgust.

"Yeah, we have a problem with that plan," Sebille Rhonda said. "Even if we could figure out a way to get Faux Lea to contact Queen Sindra, we'd have to release everyone from the Banshee scream to do it."

"And with a dragon and a giant ready to rip everything apart, there's no way I'm doing that."

I contracted my fat squishiness into a despondent puddle in the bottom of the tank. We were doomed.

"Why do you suppose whoever it was used this particular spell?" Grym asked.

Sebille Rhonda shrugged. "Probably because we have no idea who's here and who isn't."

The truth of her words sank deep. I looked at her, feeding my horror through my gaze.

It probably just looked like Slimy's normal blank gaze.

"Someone's in the artifact library doing something bad."

She nodded. "Whoever it is will have your magic and your muscle memory on how to use it."

Slimy slug slippers! We needed to reverse the spell.

"Does the frog have any inherent magic?" Grym Peabody asked.

I thought about his question. Slimy had once had magic, when my friend Rustin the ghost witch was driving the squishy green bus, a.k.a. squatting inside the frog. Madeline Quilleran, a powerful witch and Rustin's aunt had explained that the frog had soaked up some of that magic from Rustin being inside him.

But Slimy hadn't spoken since Rustin disappeared after we'd captured Margot Quilleran.

Sebille threw me a speculative look. "You might as well try, Naida. Maybe Slimy soaked up some of your magic too. He seems to be a magic sponge of some sort."

She was right. It was worth a try.

7

SIFTING MAGIC THROUGH THE SQUISH

I closed my eyes, instinctively searching for the core of magic where I usually found it.

It wasn't there.

But something answered my call. Something flared in the amphibian shell I was wearing. A silvery light sifted through me, reaching through the outer shell of the frog and coloring the air in a shifting glow that filled the tank.

I tested the power, seeking familiar magic within the mix, and felt an answering swell of energy that rose to flare inside my mind.

With a start, I realized I could see the artifacts in my mind. Not all of them. The power wasn't fully realized, but it was there, in a nascent form that felt as if it could grow.

What if I could access the magic from the artifacts? Maybe I could burn the invading spell away with that.

Unfortunately, I was afraid to try. I wasn't a Sorceress in my current form. I was a tiny amphibian. My control over the magic was limited at best. I'd only used the full force of it a couple of times. And if I pulled too hard...took too much...I risked exploding Mr. Slimy into a thousand teeny green parts.

I couldn't risk that.

But maybe there was something I *could* do.

I tugged on the edges of the small window I had, expanding it until I could see the main area of the artifact library. I slid my internal gaze along the rows of artifacts, finding a hole in the spot where Blackbeard's sword usually lay. No surprise there. It was probably stuck in the door between the spaces, trying to meet up with SB in the store.

I ran my internal vision over the rare book area, along the larger artifacts stored in the center of the open space. Then, with some trepidation, I slid it toward the toxic magic vault.

The vault door was closed, the telltale glow of the magical locking system still in place.

That was a relief.

I scanned each massive row of shelves looking for anything that was out of place.

Something moved along the floor. Two somethings, actually. Small and lithe and quick.

Hex and Wicked were pressed against the base of the shelves, moving slowly and silently.

Stalking something.

My pulse sped.

I scanned my internal vision up the end shelving unit and saw that everything seemed to be in place. Then the next section. And the next one. And finally...

There I was. Clambering up the shelving units like a giant, brown-haired spider. Whoever had taken my body was using my magic in a way I'd never known it could be used. I marveled for just a moment, examining the possibilities, and then shoved the thought aside to deal with our current problem. Faux me was scanning the shelves with something. It looked like an oversized book light that shed a soft purple glow over the items on the shelves.

A seeking rod. I recognized the artifact because I had one like it in the library.

The imposter appeared to be searching for a particular artifact.

Something flashed across the top of the shelving unit in the window of my mind, weaving an impression of red and green on the air as it shot past.

Was that Hobs?

Faux me stopped suddenly, gaze darting upward.

I held my breath, praying to the goddess that the imposter wouldn't investigate the movement overhead. I couldn't afford for faux me to see who was stalking them.

I had an idea.

I thought Wicked's name, pushing it through the magic in his direction.

Wicked paused in his stalking. His head came up as he felt the magic.

Distract, I told him through the same energy channel.

Wicked hesitated another beat, his tail snapping with uncertainty. Then he moved out of the shadows and yowled, lifting all the hair on his back and hissing as faux me looked down on him.

I need that seeking rod, I told my cat. *Find Hobs*.

The magic faltered, my window into the library folding in at the edges and growing black. I came out of it with a sense of frustration I could only dispel by flinging myself at the smeary glass.

Being a frog was a Gargoyle's stony, pointed elbows. "Ribbit!"

"Did you get anything?" Rhonda Sebille asked. "Yeah, fake me is climbing the shelves like a spider trying to find something. The cats are stalking her/him/it, and I think Hobs is there too. I saw something flash by overhead, leaving a Looney Tunes kind of cartoon trail behind."

"What do you think they're looking for?" Grym asked.

"I have an idea," I said. "But, if you don't mind,

I'd like to keep it to myself for now. I don't know who's who right now, and I don't even trust myself."

He nodded, frowning, clearly taking my caution personally. I didn't really care. He'd betrayed me before, squealing about me to the Société of Dire Magic. I wasn't going to give him any more ammunition.

"We need to go get my mother," Rhonda Sebille said.

"I'll go," the parrot said.

"There's no way you're flying through that mess out there," Grym Peabody responded. "You'll lose your way in seconds and freeze to death."

I shook my head. "SB's already dead. But there's a better than average chance she'll be disoriented and lost until the snow stops."

Silence fell between us as we all stared out the window. We were under total white-out conditions, and I could see snow building above the sill of the big window. At the rate it was falling it would soon cover the windows and doors.

"The Book of Pages!" Sebille said. "It will take us right into the greenhouse."

"Great idea!" I agreed. "But how are we going to get it? We don't know where you are, and fake me is inside the library."

She shrugged. "It's been like a sieve all night. Maybe it will just open." Without warning, she reached into the tank and scooped me up.

I screamed, "Ribbit!" as the firm surface dropped out from under me, and my stomach twisted with instant Vertigo. "Give a frog some warning!" I snapped out.

Rhonda's eyes traveled 'round the world again. The Banshee was going to wonder why her eye muscles were sore if she ever got them back.

Rhonda Sebille carried me to the door and reached for the handle. It refused to turn. "No good. You try." She held me up to the knob and I looked at it. I was pretty sure frogs couldn't just reach out and touch something. My legs didn't feel like they'd extend in that direction. "Move me closer."

She held me right over the handle, lowering me so that my back feet rested on the handle. I tried to tug the residual string of keeper power forward.

Nothing happened. "I got nothing."

Rhonda Sebille sighed. "This is a fluttercluck."

I would have nodded in agreement, but frogs couldn't nod. So I croaked instead.

Being a frog was slug-slurping fun in a spin cycle.

SB flew over and landed on Theo's upright, unmoving hand. "We need to find your body, Sebille."

"Where could it be?" Grym Peabody asked.

All eyes slid to the closed bathroom door. Then back to Sebille Rhonda.

She paled. "I don't remember. I might have been

in there. If I am, I don't want the whole world to know what I was doing."

I really wished I could roll my eyes. "Let's go check. Tell Peeping Peabody over there to stay back."

Sebille shared my message, with an edge of violence in her tone that had been distinctly missing in my original instructions. And she and I headed for the bathroom door.

It was locked.

"Porcupine poop!" Sebille screamed. "What else could go wrong? This is the worst holiday party ever. We're cursed. We're mismatched. And we're about to be smashed, fried and eaten by two gigantic mythical creatures. It's worse than my last blind date."

A small, bent piece of metal appeared in front of Sebille's raging face. She blinked at Grym Peabody, who was trying really hard not to grin.

"Blind date wasn't good, huh? Let me guess, he tried to steal a bite of your dessert?"

Sebille snatched the slim metal bar from his fingers, rage wafting off her like heat off a summer highway. "I mean, who does that?"

Grym laughed softly. "Did you turn him into a cockroach?"

She inserted the metal into the doorknob, jiggling. "Nah. It was my favorite restaurant. I didn't want to get it closed down by the health department. So, I stabbed his hand with my fork instead."

He nodded as if that made perfect sense.

Sebille tugged the bathroom door open and squealed, slamming it shut again. "We aren't ever going to be able to unsee that, are we?" she asked.

I stared blankly in her direction. "Eye bleach, please."

"Well, at least we found Earline."

The front door slammed open and a short, round figure covered in white stumbled through, falling flat on his face a few feet from the door. He lay there quivering as Grym ran over and closed the door, then knelt beside him. "Sir? Are you okay?"

The small figure shuddered violently. His bright red fingers twitching against the rug.

Grym turned him over and brushed snow from his face.

The skin of his round face was bright red like his fingers, the bulbous nose nearly purple from the cold. He opened his lips, trying to talk, but nothing came out.

"It's Eattle. Earline was right. He did go outside." I felt guilty knowing that we could have maybe brought him back before he nearly froze to death. "How in the world did he stay alive out there?"

Grym felt the Elf's skin under his thick red coat. "He's cold but not frozen. He hasn't been out there that long."

He must have taken shelter somewhere.

Sebille set me down on the floor and hurried over to the coat closet. She came back with several coats, draping them over the man. "I'll make him some hot tea," she said.

Eattle's lips opened and he forced out a single, shaky word. "Eerrliine?"

I grimaced.

"She's um, fine," Sebille Rhonda said.

He seemed to relax, closing his eyes. He didn't say anything else. In fact, he appeared to be asleep.

"Can this night get any crazier?" Grym asked.

I squatted, miserable and silent on the rug. I was pretty sure it couldn't.

8

EVERYBODY'S MIXED UP AND IT'S ALL SO CONFUSING

*W*hen I'm wrong, I like to do it up big. Like world-ending level wrong.

A shrill screaming rent the air, its terrified tones bringing the hairs up on the back of my neck. Scratch that. It would have brought the hairs up if I wasn't trapped in a frog suit.

I cast my bulgy black gaze toward the source of the sound and found a Gargoyle flailing around, mouth open wide and dark eyes filled with terror.

"What's happening? What's happening? Why am I built like a retaining wall?"

Oh, oh. The Banshee's scream spell was breaking.

"Ribbit! Ribbit! Ribbit!"

More shrieking sounded from behind the book-shelves.

"I've got this." Grym Peabody took off toward the

sound of shrieking, diving into the bookshelves and disappearing. I started hopping in that direction but discovered the muscle memory in the frog suit wasn't all it was cracked up to be. I must have pushed harder with one back leg than the other because I veered wildly off course, doing a full belly splat against the side of a shelf and sliding down to the rug with a muffled croak.

I lay on the carpet for a beat, imaginary horse-flies circling my head, and then uncrossed my eyes and pushed back to my webbed feet.

Let's try this again, I thought. What I actually said was, "Ribbit."

I did a small, tentative hop and hit hard, falling over. I mentally adjusted my technique and tried again, gaining a bit more distance and staying on my feet.

I smiled inwardly. I could do this frog thing. But I had a new respect for Rustin.

It wasn't easy being green.

I hopped again, testing my limits and then tried stringing two hops together. I was gearing up for a massive finish when something goosed me and I was suddenly clamped inside a pair of giant hands, hurtling skyward.

Whoa! "Ribbit!"

"Sorry," Sebille Rhonda bellowed into my sensi-tive froggy ear canals. Then she grimaced and my green face turned pink.

"You peed on me!" Sebille exclaimed.

I tried to fold into a tiny, green and pink-cheeked ball in the center of her hand. But there was no place to hide.

Ahead of us, in the central seating area, Grym stood with a hand on a sobbing Hobs.

Worry filled my chest. If Hobs had been affected by the spell, what had I seen skimming stealthily across the shelves in the artifact library?

By process of elimination, I figured out that the creature who looked like Hobs was probably Claudette Baxter.

The woman eyed me with a level of disgust before lifting her oversized blue Hobs eyes to Grym. "Has someone been turned into a frog?" She lifted her small hands, flexing the spidery fingers as a fresh spate of tears slid from her eyes. "I never believed in witches until today." She turned to Grym, whom she no doubt thought was Mr. Peabody. Wrapping the extra-long fingers around Grym's wrist, she leaned close, speaking in an urgent, fear-filled voice. "Who is it? Who's the witch?"

Grym Peabody covered her hand with his own. "There are no witches. It's just a bad dream. You're going to be fine."

The woman shook her head, clearly not buying what Grym was selling.

A *whoomph* sounded on the air. I turned my

beady gaze to Grym Peabody. Fortunately, I didn't have to tell him what I was thinking. Sebille Rhonda screamed it for me.

"The dragon's breaking out of the spell."

Grym and Sebille took off running, screeching to a stop as Lea Slimy hopped from between two shelves and stopped right in front of us. She turned her blank gaze in our direction and worked her throat, her tongue snapping out to snag a spider from the wooden end wall of the shelf.

Ew! I decided, when it was all over, I wouldn't tell Lea what she'd done as Mr. Slimy. It would be a kindness.

We dodged around her and started running as another *whoomph* sound throbbed on the air.

My innards bounced up and down and my brain felt like it was in a blender as Sebille clomped heavily along the carpet as if she was still wearing her Wicked Witch of the West shoes.

Hm. I'd always blamed the ill-fitting shoes. Maybe it had been Sebille all along.

We rounded the front shelving unit and Sebille screeched to a stop, Grym barely stopping himself before barreling into the back of us.

The dragon's head was turning, its beautiful gaze taking in its surroundings as if it was still half asleep.

The giant's back was to us, but I thought I'd seen his head move a titch. It was going to be a race to see which of them gained full capacities first.

"See if you can talk to her before she goes off again," I told Sebille.

My assistant clomped over and stood in front of the dragon, the elegant head swiveled in our direction, a pair of opaline eyes, almond-shaped and exquisitely beautiful, focused on me first and then on Sebille Rhonda. There was fear in the eyes.

"Ask her who she is," I told Sebille.

The Sprite reached out and touched the dragon's quivering silver side. "It's okay. We'll fix this. You'll be fine as long as you stay calm."

The eyes closed briefly, the small ears twitching. "What's happened to me, dear?"

Mrs. Foxladle, I thought, with a feeling of sadness. She seemed so fragile, so human, what if the shock of the spell hurt her? Or worse? Anger slid through me, I suddenly wanted to get my hands on whoever had released the spell. I wasn't sure what I'd do to them, but boxing their ears wasn't going to be enough to make me feel better.

Maybe I'd lock them in a room with Sebille for a few hours.

Sebille smiled, the effect more soothing in Rhonda's face than it would have been in Sebille's. The Sprite was all sharp angles and acidic purpose. Nothing about her ever soothed. "Mrs. Foxladle?"

The dragon nodded.

"If you'll just trust us, we'll fix this. I promise."

The dragon frowned. "Who are you, dear?"

"I'm..." Sebille closed her mouth, apparently deciding not to say what she'd been about to say. "I'm just a friend."

The Gargoyle's head moved with the creak of rock against rock. A determined gaze found mine. "I'm trying to keep her safe," he ground out. "What happened?"

I recognized the inflections in the familiar voice. "Theo?"

The Gargoyle nodded. "Somebody spelled us."

I nodded. "It's probably in the food."

He frowned. "All I ate were cookies."

I thought of the insatiable appetite everyone seemed to have for those frosted sugar cookies. And the residual drunkenness. The spell had to be in the cookies. "We'll fix it. We just need to find someone who can rework the spell."

"Theo?" a faint voice asked. Faux Mrs. Foxladle put a hand on the Gargoyle's blocky arm. "Is that you in there?"

Theo Grym nodded, eyeing the elderly woman with confusion. "Birte?"

"Yes. Why are you a Gargoyle? And why am I...?" She looked down at herself and frowned. "Old?"

"It's an identity mixing hex," Sebille Rhonda offered. "We're working on reversing it now. We just need everybody to stay calm."

The floor behind us creaked. Sebille whipped around and we looked up, up, up into the giant's

slowly opening eyes. Rage flared through them
when he saw us, and then eased into something that
looked more like pain. "What..." he stopped, licked
his lips. "What's going on?"

"Devard," Sebille Rhonda told me. "Someone's
spelled us. I know you're discombobulated, Devard,
but you need to rein in your baser instincts and stay
calm. We're all trapped here, and I can't have you
hurting people."

Devard Theo grunted, but he seemed to have
understood her warning.

"What is he?" I whispered to Sebille.

"Naga," she said out of the corner of her mouth.

I felt my froggy eyes go wide. *Yikes! An ancient
snake monster.* I'd have to be sure and be nicer to him
in the future.

A ratty feather sifted down as the parrot flew
overhead to land on Sebille's shoulder. "The giant be
a fair bet to beat the Gods of Winter, Lass," Lea SB
said.

I sighed. "Translation, please?"

"I think she's suggesting we send Devard Theo to
the greenhouse to fetch my mother. We need a Fae
to reverse this spell."

"Ah," I said with a froggy smile. "I like that idea."
Ribbit!

"He's too big to get through the door," Grym Peabody said, eyeing the giant. When he'd been transformed into Theo, Devard had somehow ended up in a size that was halfway between his normal, human-facing seven feet tall, and his full-on giant size of about thirty feet tall. "How are we going to get him out?"

We all stared at the front door. Short of blasting a giantnormous hole in the front of the building, we weren't getting Devard through the front.

"We can let him out the back door," I suggested to Sebille. There was a garage-sized door in the back for larger artifacts.

My assistant nodded. "But we'll never get him through the dividing door."

She was right. I really didn't want to bash a hole through that door and open the library up to everyone.

"If you had your keeper powers, you could stretch it," Sebille suggested.

If only.

Theo Grym gently settled the now calm dragon to the floor. "I'll go get the queen," he said. "This body will make it through the snow, and I don't think it will freeze easily."

Standing next to him in Mr. Peabody's form, Grym nodded. "He's right. He won't freeze and he's heavy enough to plow through any amount of snow out there."

"Okay, it's settled then," Sebille said.

Theo Grym nodded and headed for the front door. He walked past the wet spot on the carpet where Eattle had been.

The Elf was gone.

"Hey, did anybody see where Eattle went?" I croaked.

Lea twisted SB's head, her beady black eyes scouring the room. "The scalawag's debunked."

Frowning, Sebille shook her head. "He was there a minute ago."

The sound of a toilet flushing brought all our gazes to the bathroom door. It opened a beat later and Earline walked out. She jerked to a stop, seeing everybody staring at her. Finally, she said. "Is this the line for the bathroom? I didn't think I was in there *that* long."

She had no idea.

Earline walked away and headed for the food table.

Sebille Rhonda's face folded into a horrified grimace.

"What's wrong?" I asked her, watching Earline stick a pudgy hand into the bowl of potato chips.

"She didn't even wash her hands."

I would have grimaced if I could have. Instead, I had to settle for a croak of disgust. *No chips for me.*

Grym tugged Sebille aside. "Okay, we hopefully have help on the way for the identity mixing spell. I think we've got everybody settled down. What do we need to get control of next?"

"Ribbit!"

Grym looked down on me with Mr. Peabody's mild gaze. "What did she say?"

I really wished the Gargoyle could understand amphibian.

Sebille sighed. "She said we need to get into the artifact library. Somebody stole her body and was looking for something in there. Whoever it is, they spelled us to keep us from discovering which of us was missing and they could be taking off right now with a stolen artifact. Given the weather and the general chaos we're currently experiencing, we're going to be seriously late to the game and struggling to catch up by the time we figure out who it is."

Grym arched Peabody's shaggy gray-brown brows. "She said all that with just one Ribbit, huh?"

Sebille put Rhonda's eye muscles through another circuit.

Yep, the Banshee was definitely going to have something to scream about when she got her saggy, worn-out eyes back.

9

YET MORE BEASTIES

a thunderous roar shook the walls.

Sebille and Grym whipped around and Sebille's hands tightened on my squishy body.

She loosened her grip when I made a constricted croaking sound. "What was that?"

Behind us, the giant straightened to his full height. His fist clenched. "Death," he said, his lip curling.

We were all silent for a moment. Finally, I asked, "Did he say death?"

Grym frowned at me. "I wish that frog could talk."

"Yes," Sebille ground out through clenched teeth. "He said death." She turned to Devard Theo. "Explain."

"As you can imagine, I have to keep my magical form tightly bound. It's unmanageable and unstable.

I'm afraid this spell might have released the Naga. While my spirit is in this giant's form, my body became the Naga. It's not going to be happy with the magical shenanigans."

Raging reptiles!

We all took a moment to let that sink in. My little froggy heart was pounding against my chest like a "too stupid to live" teenage girl pounds on the door of the haunted house at midnight at Halloween.

Another roar shook the building. The bookshelves creaked as something really big pressed against them. I watched in horror as a massive form uncoiled at the back of the store. The monster had a body that was bigger around than Grym in his Gargoyle form and a head...

I swallowed hard.

"Slithering snake fangs," I murmured. "We're toast."

The serpent oozed forward, its ten-foot-long head resting on top of the third bookshelf from the back and its body slithering up behind it.

The shelves groaned and wobbled as the enormous monster crept across their tops, its slanted eyes fixed hungrily on us and the slits of its nostrils flaring with interest.

Mrs. Foxladle lost her hard-won composure, her wings pounding in panic as she backpedaled toward the food table near the counter. She crashed into it and bellowed out a panicked cry tinged with smoke. I knew fire was just behind the smoke.

I looked at Sebille. "Do something?"

"I can immobilize everybody again, but you and Grym will be caught this time."

The snake reached the front shelf and the head slid sideways, eyeing Lea, who was hopping around near the front door. The thick body tensed, preparing to strike. The long, forked tongue slipped out to test the air, scenting its prey.

"No!" I screamed. *RibbitRibbitRibbitRibbit!!*

Grym Peabody lunged into the center of the room, waving his arms. "Here snakey, snakey! Come and get me."

The snake complied, the head whipping forward so quickly I was afraid Grym wouldn't have time to move out of the way.

He leaped sideways, hitting the ground behind the sales counter as the enormous fangs slammed into the top of the counter, piercing the granite surface like it was made of paper, and retracting with an angry hiss.

A thick yellow substance seeped down the front of the counter, sizzling like acid.

The head swung back toward Lea.

"Scream!" I yelled at Sebille.

She tugged up her sweater, wrapping it around me in a smothering cocoon, and yelled Grym's name in warning.

The bladed sound of the Banshee's scream was dulled by the sweater and, judging by the pressure against my frame, Sebille's hands.

Even beneath my protective cocoon, I could feel the undeniable power of the banshee's scream pulsing against my skull. As before, unrelenting pressure filled my head until it felt like it would explode.

Since I'd experienced it before, I knew about when the sound would change. I counted the frantic beats of my heart as I waited for it to happen. After a long moment, the sound dulled to a throb...the final push...pulsing darkly until my brain felt soft.

The throbbing eased into a low, rhythmic hum at last. I went limp in Sebille's hands, fighting to slow my frantically pounding heart.

After a moment, I realized it wasn't my heart that was pounding.

There was a long moment of stillness before Sebille slowly unwound me. I waited in fear, terrified of what I'd see when the store was revealed.

As the fabric was pulled away, I found myself staring into fangs as long as Sebille's arm, dripping acid onto the rug at her feet.

The Naga was mere inches away, its snaky face filled with the promise of death.

That had been close.

I gulped as the carpet sizzled and burned below me.

Slowly lifting my gaze to Sebille, I saw the terror mirrored in the unfamiliar brown depths of Rhonda's eyes. The white of the Naga's fangs were mirrored in her eyes, giving them the appearance of a reptilian gaze.

"Banshee bloomers," Sebille breathed out. "He almost got me."

The front door blew open and Theo Grym stumbled inside, a blast of frigid air blowing snow inside with him and turning the carpet white in an inverted vee in front of the door.

He held a duffle bag in one hand and wiped a thick layer of snow from his face with the other. "It's like Hades out there, if Hades was cold instead of hot," he said.

"Did you get mother?" Sebille asked. She dodged around the snake and ran to him, taking the duffel he handed to her.

Sebille set it on the ground and unzipped it. A column of dragonfly-sized Sprites fluttered out, the illumination of their iridescent, multi-colored wings flashing as they spread out around the space.

Queen Sindra flew over and hovered before the snake, her tiny face filled with wonder. "A Naga? How is that possible?"

"It was bound by my friend Devard."

Sindra flew over the snake's head and along its length, studying it as if she were a tiny, flying scientist who'd just made a major discovery. When she returned to us, she shook her head. "I'm not sure what we're going to do with this."

"Can we rebind it?" Sebille asked.

We all looked at the giant, who was now Devard, but he was glassy-eyed and unmoving, caught in the Banshee's spell.

"Maybe it will return to its host when the identity mixing spell is reversed," I offered.

Sindra eyed me. "Naida?"

"Ribbit," I affirmed.

She grinned. "You look good in green."

"I'll be honest," I told her, "It's not my favorite color."

She chuckled.

Sebille explained our situation to her mother.

Sindra listened, her guards flickering rapidly around the store, checking out my immobile guests. When Sebille finished, the queen nodded her understanding. "First things first. Let's reverse this spell. Then we'll need to make sure your human guests are comfortable..." She lifted tiny blonde brows at me.

I got her meaning. We'd have to wipe their memory of the whole mess.

"Ribbit," I said in agreement.

"Then you'll be able to go see what's happening in the library."

With the plan set, I felt better. However, there would be new problems if whoever had visited the

Universe's equivalent of Hades on us at my Holiday party managed to find the artifact they were looking for and absconded with it.

I mentally checked myself. One thing at a time. It was all my little froggy heart could handle.

Sindra looked at Sebille, I wondered how she'd recognized her so easily. I made a mental note to ask. Later. "Do you have any ideas how the spell was spread?"

"The frosted cookies," I told Sebille.

She nodded. "That's what I was thinking too. They were doused with a spell to make them irresistible. There's only one reason for someone to do that."

"If they wanted to make sure everybody had one," I croaked in agreement.

"Who brought those cookies?" Sindra asked.

Sebille looked down at me. I thought about shrugging, but my little squishy shoulders wouldn't comply. "Mrs. Foxladle brought a tin of cookies."

Sebille shook her head. "Not her."

I agreed. "Devard?"

Sebille's negative response was a beat slow. "I don't know why Devard would want to spell us."

"Maybe he's still mad at you for turning that guy into a slug."

She shrugged. "I don't think so. Besides, he spelled himself."

That *did* seem to be a point in his favor. "Theo

and Birte brought cookies too," I said reluctantly. I didn't want to blame the giant. He was my friend. But in the interests of getting to the bottom of the current mess, I had to face the facts. "I suppose it's possible he wanted something from the library."

"But you said you saw yourself climbing the stacks, searching. Theo's been here, in the form of the Gargoyle, all along."

Yes. He had.

"I'm at a loss," I told my assistant.

"Okay, let's see if we can read the spell on those cookies," Sindra said.

"Can you do that?" I asked as Sebille started toward the destroyed food table. Earline was bending toward the ground, one stubby hand reaching for the meatballs that were spilled across the carpet.

Ew!

"If it's a Fae spell, we can," Sebille told me.

"Which cookies were they?" Sindra asked. She buzzed back and forth above the broken cookies spilled on the floor.

They all looked alike when they were broken.

Sebille bent over them too, frowning. "I don't know."

"They smelled like sugar and vanilla," I told Sebille.

"That was the lure," she said, her eyes widening. "But it should still be there." She set me down on the ground and went to her knees, sniffing the mounds of broken cookies.

After a minute, she pulled a nearly intact bell-shaped frosted cookie from one pile and sniffed it, her eyes going glazed. She was opening her mouth to eat it when Sindra flew over and whacked her on the nose with a wing.

Sebille blinked, her face folding into a glower. "Ow, that hurt!"

"You'll thank me tomorrow," Sindra said. She held her hands over the cookie and a soft, green glow emanated from her palms. The energy bathed the cookie, surrounded it, and covered it in tiny, crisscrossing lines like you'd see on a graph.

The lines blurred and thickened and then thinned back out and settled into place, a series of strange symbols floating above the different segments of the cookie.

"Here's the lure," Sindra said. She wiggled her fingers over the cookie and lifted her hand, drawing the magic from the surface of the cookie like a shimmering spider web and flinging it away.

The magic that was left coalesced into the irregular shape of the frosting, covering it with raised symbols that glowed a vibrant purple above the chunk of cookie.

Sindra's gaze lifted to Sebille's. "Purple," she said.

Sebille frowned.

"What does that mean?" I asked Sebille.

She shook her head.

Sindra wiggled her fingers over the symbols, and some of them lifted away. She gathered them in her palm and, examining the remaining symbols carefully, settled each one in a different spot on the surface, nudging a few aside to insert new ones, and placing several of them at the front and back of the existing spell.

Finally, she buzzed higher into the air, looking down at the results. Then she covered the entire thing with a sparkling green layer of her own, distinctive magic. "That should do it." She pointed to Grym Peabody. "Give him a small piece of the cookie."

Grym was immobilized, but his lips were parted. Sebille settled me onto the floor and plucked the chunk of cookie from the air. She broke the cookie and stuffed a piece between his lips.

We waited a beat...and then another one...and Mr. Peabody blinked, his arms dropping to his sides. He scanned a look toward Sebille, blinked again, and then focused on Sindra. His eyes went wide. "Is that a Fairy?"

It had worked!

Sebille gave Birte a bite of the cookie and the dragon came to, her eyes filled with surprise but no fear. She quickly returned to her human form and ducked into the bathroom with a squeal.

"There's a robe hanging on the door," Sebille called out to her.

Grym had come back to himself when Mr. Peabody returned. He didn't return to his human form, probably because he had no clothes to put on.

Mrs. Foxladle wandered to the front of the store, looking perplexed but otherwise normal.

SB squawked enthusiastically, taking to the air in a messy jumble of shedding feathers and blue language.

I didn't need a pirate translator to know he was annoyed by his recent loss of body. I didn't know where he'd gone while Lea held his body, but I guessed, since he was technically dead, he'd waited in the ether somewhere until she'd vacated his skin.

Claudette took one look at the crowd of people and the state of the store and her knees buckled, sending her into a chair near the front window.

"What about Lea?" I croaked.

Sebille shook her head. "We can't release her yet. Rhonda either. Not until you and I find our bodies."

She was right. If we released Slimy from Lea and Rhonda...

We both looked around, wondering where Rhonda had gone. "She's missing too," I told Sebille.

The Sprite sighed. "We'll deal with that after we find our bodies." She nodded toward the snake. "I don't know what's going to happen with the Naga.

Things might go badly. I'm inclined to wait on that transformation until you and I are fixed."

"If you take a bite, you should return to your body," I told her.

She shook her head. "Whoever set the spell took us somewhere. I don't want to reactivate us until I know where our bodies are."

As anxious as I was to get back to normal, I had to admit she was right.

Birte came out of the bathroom. "What about Theo?"

Sebille looked at me.

"We need our magic," I said.

Sebille nodded. "We can't release him just yet. Naida and I need to find our bodies so we can help restrain the Naga if it goes bad."

She scanned Theo a quick glance, then took in the snake. Understanding lit her gaze. "Okay. I'll stand guard here. If things go south, my dragon can hold the Naga off until you get back."

"Thanks, Birte." If my little froggy arms... legs?...had been long enough, I would have hugged her.

Sebille looked at the connecting door and nodded to her mother. "Will you see if you can unwind the spell on the lock?"

10

TEENY, TINY AMPHIBIAN DIAPERS

*T*he artifact library was too quiet. I expected the cats to assault us as soon as we opened the door, but they were nowhere to be seen. I had a sudden flare of panic that the imposter had hurt them, and raised my bulgy black gaze to Sebille Rhonda. "I'm going to try to sense the cats."

She nodded and settled my squishy self onto Shakespeare's desk.

The leather blotter warmed and rolled beneath my wide, green butt and I hopped in surprise, emitting a startled croak.

Sebille arched a brow at the suspicious trail of liquid I'd left behind. If I hadn't been cold-blooded in that moment, I would have surely gotten heated cheeks.

Well...actually...I had gotten heated cheeks. Just

not the ones on my face. "This frog bus needs tiny little depends."

Sebille chuckled darkly.

I reached for the wisps of energy infused in the frog's cells, tugging them slowly forward and coalescing them as best I could without a real sense of control or focus.

When I had a core of energy gathered, I sent my thoughts outward, picturing my form and Sebille's.

A soft clang danced across the open space. Sebille and I shared a surprised look. The magic had found an artifact. But I hadn't been looking for one.

"It came from upstairs," Sebille said, pointing toward my apartment at the top of the stairs. She scooped me up and ran lightly up the steps, turning my tiny froggy brain to mush in the process.

I was dizzy and nauseous from the bouncing around by the time she reached the landing.

"Be careful," I warned. "We don't know what's waiting in there for us."

She nodded without giving me her patented Sebille glower. That was when I knew how discombobulated my assistant was from everything that had happened.

Grym's voice called out behind us. Sebille turned to shush him.

I heard his heavy footsteps climbing the steps. The sound was a comfort. I might still be peeved at him, but he was a good man to have in my corner in a fight.

Sebille hesitated another moment.

I realized with a start that she was scared. In all the years I'd known the Sprite, I'd only seen her show fear a couple of times. The reality made my little froggy limbs tremble.

Without looking down, Sebille curled Rhonda's lips. "If you pee on me, I'm going to make you eat bugs."

I attempted a few frantic Kegel exercises in hopes of heading off disaster. But I couldn't find any muscles to tighten.

Nope. Zero bladder control. Sebille was playing with fire by even holding me.

Sucked to be her.

"What's happening?" Grym asked, trying to peer around Sebille and through the open door.

"The frog is about to pee on me again, and I'm going to hurt her if she does."

Grym grinned down at me. "Again, huh?"

"Stop talking," I said. But all he heard was, "Ribbit!"

He chuckled as if he'd understood me.

"She sent out her keeper energy and something clanged up here," Sebille said.

Grym nodded. "Let's go see what it was."

Just that easy.

Alrighty then.

Sebille shoved Grym through the door first. She might be cocky and nearly fearless. But she wasn't stupid.

He took a few steps and stopped, his big form going perfectly still.

Something was wrong.

Something was horribly wrong.

Trickle. Trickle. Trickle.

"Ew!" The Sprite held me away from her with a horrified grimace. I sent a quick prayer to the goddess that she didn't fling me across the room.

"Sorry! This squishy green package isn't very hardy."

"You owe me lunch for a week," Sebille said, still grimacing.

"Done," I said, wincing internally. But it wasn't going to be bugs.

Rubbing her wet hand on poor Rhonda's dress, Sebille stepped forward. Her foot thumped against something. We looked down at the seeking rod the imposter had been using. It was lying on my carpet.

"I guess we found the artifact that clanged," I told my assistant.

She nodded and walked into the apartment, her head on a swivel. Her gaze finally followed Grym's and stopped as his had. The two of them were motionless.

I strained to see past the big Detective. "Ribbit!"

Sebille stepped sideways, giving me a clear view of the object of their horror.

Or should I say objects?

I croaked pitifully.

It was my body and Sebille's. We were flung across the bed like discarded clothing, our limbs tangled and bent at odd angles. Our open eyes were black, empty, and our flesh was collapsed, like woman-shaped pillows that had been de-stuffed and rejected.

Wicked and Hex lay nearby on the bed as if keeping watch on our corpses. When he saw us, Mr. Wicked lifted his head and gave us a plaintive yowl.

I realized in that moment my cat believed I was gone.

It just about broke my heart.

My little froggy form shuddered violently. It was a singularly unjolly sight.

Finally, Grym turned to Sebille, all trace of fun missing from his handsome face. "You brought the cookie?"

Sebille nodded, her gaze locked on the disturbing sight before her.

"Sebille?" I said.

She seemed transfixed. Rhonda's face was slack with horror.

"Sebille!"

Nothing. Her mind seemed as empty as the shell of her body.

What if her mind had fled at the sight of her sunken, empty form? What if the imposter had left a spell in my apartment that stole her very essence? Would I be next? Grym? I panicked. "Sebille! I feel another pee coming on!"

The Sprite blinked, opened her eyes wide, and shoved a piece of cookie into my mouth.

She quickly set me on the floor and took a bite of what was left just as the world started spinning around me and my small, incontinent body fell away.

Waves of energy swirled around me. Purple waves that dove into my nooks and crevices and tugged at my flesh, shoving, plumping, and prodding me until it filled me to the brim, and then slowly receding. The energy left behind a slight ringing in my ears and a sour taste in my mouth.

Smacking my lips against the horrible taste, I opened my eyes and found myself staring at a familiar gray stain on the ceiling above my bed.

It had worked! I clenched my fingers and curled my toes, checking all my limbs to make sure they worked. My body felt heavy, swollen, and I figured that was probably because I'd been a frog for so long and had to adjust back to being normal size.

The bed moved, and I remembered I wasn't alone. I slowly turned my head and looked into Sebille's shining green gaze.

I'd never seen anything so beautiful in my life.

We shared a smile, and Sebille reached out to clasp my hand in a tight, almost desperate grip.

I was touched by the act until I felt the cold, wet sliminess in her palm.

Her eyes turned hostile. "You will never pee on me again."

I jerked my hand away, grimacing. "It wasn't my fault."

"Meow!" Wicked flung himself at me, purring so loudly it rumbled in my chest as he rubbed along my sides.

"Hey, buddy. I'm sorry I scared you."

He rubbed his head against my chin, flopping down to roll around the mattress next to me. Hex came over and gave me a tentative nudge with her soft head, her dark gold gaze filled with concern.

I scratched behind her ears. "It's all good, pretty girl."

Sebille shoved upright, wobbling slightly before pushing to her feet. "Stop dallying, Naida. We have a thief to find."

If Sebille wobbled a bit on her ugly red shoes, it didn't take away from her exit. She held her head high, like the Sprite Princess she was, and moved quickly away from us, through the door.

I was a little surprised she didn't run over to the sink to wash her hands.

That was the first thing I was going to do. The artifact thief could wait. I wasn't walking around with frog pee on my hands. A girl had to have her priorities.

"Are you sure this is where you saw faux you climbing around?"

I nodded, my gaze scouring the shelves rising forty feet above our heads. "There's nothing missing." Back in my own body, I'd wasted no time reaching for my keeper magic and taking a quick inventory of the library. "There's nothing missing anywhere. What do you suppose they were doing here?"

"Just because nothing's missing doesn't mean they weren't looking for something," Grym reminded me. "Maybe they just haven't found it yet."

I nodded. "But, if that's true..." My eyes went wide. "They might have switched the search to the bookstore."

Grym frowned. "It's possible."

Sebille shivered. "Is anybody else cold?"

As soon as she said it, I realized I was. Rubbing my arms, I glanced around. The library kept itself at a magically perfect temperature at all times. The only way that would have changed was if the magic was down.

It wasn't down. I could feel it throbbing all around me when I reached for it.

Sebille and I had the same thought at the same time.

"The big door!" we both said at once.

We took off running around the shelves and headed for the main area of the library, Grym on our heels.

I saw the swirling eddies of snow on the concrete floor before we got close enough to see the sliver of daylight at the edge of the big sliding door.

Blustery air filtered through the two-inch crack, turning the area nearest the door cold and lowering the temperature in the remainder of the massive space by several degrees.

"The intruder left through here," Grym said. He grabbed the edge of the door and shoved it further open, stepping out into the snow.

The overhead light shone down on his dark head, and the only snow in the air was a dusting of sparkling flakes the breeze had tugged from the thick cover on the ground and sent dancing across the open lot behind Croakies.

The storm had finally stopped.

Grym pointed to an area nearest the building, under the overhang of the roof. The snow was only about six inches deep there and I saw a distinctive trail of footprints leading to the corner of the building.

Grym pointed toward that corner. "I'm going to

follow those tracks. I'll come in through the front in a few minutes."

I nodded. "We'll meet you there."

Two gray streaks shot through the door and followed Grym along the wall.

"You have Wicked and Hex," I yelled out to Grym. He lifted a hand over his head to let me know he'd heard.

Sebille and I hurried back inside, shivering. We closed and sealed the door and headed back to the front.

A tall, slender form stepped from the shadows, startling us, and we turned to find Rhonda standing near the stacks, her gaze slightly dazed. "Naida?" Her voice was weak, breathless. "I...I'm..." Rhonda wavered on her feet. We hurried over to catch her, supporting her between us. "I feel funny."

"It's okay," I told her, meeting Sebille's gaze on the other side of the Banshee. "It's all going to be all right now."

Yeah, remember what I said before about my being wrong?

We walked Rhonda toward the dividing door, the Banshee getting stronger with every step as the effects of the spell fell away. Listening to Sebille explain to her about the hex, I shoved the door open.

And came face to face with trouble.

11

THE TRUE SOUL OF CHRISTMAS

*E*attle stood by the Christmas tree, an ugly gleam in his beady black eyes.

Hobs stood a few feet away, clutching the partially unwrapped package he'd given me for Christmas.

Eattle extended a short, pudgy hand toward Hobs. "Give me the box, boy."

Hobs wrapped his arms more tightly around the wrapped gift. "No. This is Miss's box. I gave it to her."

"You stole it from me," Eattle charged.

Hobs shook his head. "It was in the throw-away bin. You didn't want it."

Oh, oh. I stepped into the room, dodging around the still-frozen snake and the immobile giant. "What's going on?" I asked the Elf.

"Your hobgoblin stole my Soul of Christmas. I followed his trail here and I want it back."

I glanced at Hobs. His gaze was watery with unshed tears, but his chin was firm. He felt he was in the right. "Hobs said you threw it out. Is that true?"

Eattle's expression changed, became wheedling. "It was a mistake, Naida keeper. You know it is, with winter cleaning and all. The Misses just pitched it by mistake. If you make the boy hand it over, I won't press charges."

"I don't make Hobs do anything," I told Eattle. "He's a free man."

Eattle's gaze went wide. "You're kidding me, right?"

"Nope." I looked at Hobs. "Where was the box when you found it, Hobs?"

"At the old lady's house," he said. "Three big, brown houses up from here. She died, Miss. And her family didn't want the box. They threw it out."

They were humans, no doubt, and had no idea what the box was. Not that it would have mattered to them if they had. The magic only worked for the magical. "So, it was never yours?" I asked the Elf.

His expression turned dark, angry. "Earline and me found that box first, and I mean to have it."

I shook my head. "If Hobs found that box in the trash, then it was fair game. I'm sorry, Eattle. But you aren't getting the box. It would be best if you and Earline left now. The storm is over."

Eattle growled.

Mrs. Foxladle stepped forward, giving the Elf a

nervous smile. "I have a music box very similar to that one if you'll consider a replacement," she told him kindly. "I just don't have any use for it."

"You don't need to do that, Mrs. Foxladle," I said. The last thing I wanted was for the mean-tempered Elf to take something the sweet elderly woman offered just to make peace. "He only wants that particular box. And he's done bad things to get it," I said, leveling a look on Eattle.

"Nobody's permanently hurt, are they?"

I glanced at the snake, which was like a giant dagger poised over all of us. "That remains to be seen," I told him. "Now, please leave and take Earline with you. You've caused enough trouble."

"Watch out!" Birte screamed.

I turned to see her running toward me, still wearing the robe and nothing else.

Cold metal found my throat. I went very still.

"Anybody moves and she dies," Earline said, her voice cold.

So there she was.

Eattle stepped closer to Hobs, twitching his outstretched hand. "If you don't want Miss to die, you'll give me the box, boy."

Hobs looked from me to Eattle. His teary blue gaze dropped to the box in his hands.

Something moved past the glass on the other side of the tree.

I looked at Hobs. "It's okay, Hobs. Do what you think is best. I'll be okay either way."

The hobgoblin stared at me for a long moment. Then he nodded, and, after giving me one last look, shot off in a blur and hit the top of the shelves, dancing from one to the next so quickly it was hard to see him move.

A beat later, a pair of keys flew through the air and hit Earline. Her head snapped back, and she grunted in pain.

A small, black purse whipped through the store and smacked Eattle in the head. He staggered backward just as the front door crashed open.

The wooden door hit the Elf so hard it sent him flying. He crashed up against the sales counter several feet away.

A Gargoyle walked into the room, his rocky form dusted white from the blowing snow.

Earline yelped in outrage as Sebille wrapped her in binding magic, and I stepped away, rubbing my throat where the blade had nicked it.

The knife hit the carpet with a dull thud.

Wicked and Hex ran over to the blade and stared down at it. The weapon disappeared in a puff of silvery energy.

Grym examined Eattle, particularly interested in his funny pointed shoes. "You know, it's a strange thing. The prints leading from the back are shaped just like these." He kicked the bottom of Eattle's shoe, his gaze rising slowly to Earline. "And there are two sets of them. One big and one small."

Surprise made me turn to look at the struggling Elf. "But how? She was here with us the whole time."

"Was she?" Grym asked. "There was a lot going on. Nobody was really keeping track, and half the time we literally didn't know who was who."

Which I realized was exactly what the Elves had hoped. "How'd she get through the door into the library?" I asked, glaring at Earline.

Queen Sindra flew from the back of the store, followed by her guards. "They overrode the keeper magic with this." She held up a key-shaped locket on a silver chain. Sindra glanced at Hobs, who was sitting atop the nearest shelf, kicking his heels against the books and twirling a finger through his red and white scarf. "The hobgoblin's been quietly pilfering stuff from everybody during the party. He's got a pile behind the last shelving unit. He must have taken this from Earline after the identity mixing spell put everybody out of commission."

I frowned. "Out of commission?"

"Yes," Sindra said. "If this spell worked the way it was drawn, you would have all been unconscious for several minutes. The Elves breached the door and put a special ward on it so they could go through any time they wanted."

I shuddered, thinking of being unaware for that long while the two nasty critters invaded Croakies.

"But where'd she get the key?" Sebille asked.

Sindra flew over and hovered before Earline, her wings beating the air with an angry rhythm. "This is ancient magic. If I'm not wrong, it came from Santa's workshop."

"Santa?" I asked. The head Elf himself.

"Of course," Grym said, nodding. "How do you think Santa gets into all those houses on Christmas Eve?"

"Down the chimney?" I said, unwilling to let the final dregs of my Santa illusion be quashed.

"What about homes that don't have chimney's?" Grym asked, kindly. I got the impression he would have gone further with his argument, probably telling me Santa was too round to fit down a chimney, but he seemed to sense my reluctance to hear the truth of that little lie.

Good man.

I put out my hand and Sindra dropped the chain with the key into it. "Thanks, Queen Sindra. The potential for this to be abused is monumental." I hoped Santa had a spare because the key was going into the toxic magic vault tout de suite.

Looking at Earline's nasty glower and hostile black gaze, I had a feeling it had already been used for evil.

"My pleasure. We dosed your human friends with a denial spell. They don't see any magic in the room or recognize any magical creatures. Everyone looks human to them."

Well, that explained why none of them was freaking out about the giant snake hovering above and behind me.

"Would you like help with that?" Sindra asked, nodding toward the Naga.

I shook my head. "We'll take care of it. Thanks so much for your help."

Inclining her head, the Fae queen and her guards headed out of the store. I hugged Mrs. Foxla-dle, Claudette, and Mr. Peabody and thanked them for coming. To my vast surprise, they all gushed about how much fun they'd had and tried to get me to commit to another party the following year.

Gargoyles would sprout wings and fly before that happened.

Closing the door behind them, I leaned against it and closed my eyes, amazed to have survived the party.

"Hey!" Lea said, looking around. "Where's Eattle?"

My eyes snapped to the spot where he'd been. All that was left was a damp Elf suit on the carpet. "What the?"

Grym crouched down and tugged the red suit off the floor.

I gasped.

It wasn't just a suit. It was a full skin.

Eattle wasn't real either?

"What by the goddess's favorite chocolate bar is going on?"

"Skinwalkers," Grym said, half under his breath. "No wonder..."

I eyed him. "Care to share with the class?"

He shook his head. "Police business. Sorry. It's an ongoing investigation."

I wanted to smack him upside the head. His "ongoing investigation" had rolled my party and my home like a heard of giants trying to get to a penny sale before it closed.

"He's got to be here somewhere," Grym said. "We need to look for him."

We searched the bookstore but didn't find any sign of the Elf. Sebille even checked the coat closet with no luck.

Birte yanked the bathroom door open and stepped inside. We heard the shower curtain snapping back and cabinets opening and closing.

I frowned. If Eattle was inside a cabinet, he had bigger problems even than we knew. Finally, Birte's voice rang out. "Found something."

Relief filled me.

Birte came out of the bathroom, carrying a duffle bag. "This was stuffed into the linen closet, covered by some towels."

She set it down on the floor and Grym unzipped it, his face losing much of its healthy color as he took in its contents. He pulled another skin suit out. It looked like Rhonda.

"There were two of them?"

But he wasn't done. The next suit looked like Earline. Then Grym. Then Hobs. There were even suits that looked like Slimy and Mr. Wicked.

"They brought extra suits for each of the people they expected to be at this party," I breathed, appalled. "They planned ahead on this."

"But when did they bring this bag inside?" Lea asked.

"Probably while we were all unconscious," Sebille offered.

I fought back another shudder. What else had they done while I was out cold?

An icy breeze made me shiver. The scent of wet fur tickled my nose. Before I had time to consider what it meant, a tall, dark shape flashed past with a deep-throated laugh. The creature resembled a seven-foot-tall wolf that stood on bent back legs which ended in hooves. Its fangs curved over a hairy chin, and its forepaws ended in deadly-looking claws. The creature slammed into me, knocking me into Grym and sending us both to the floor.

I turned my head just as the shape, really almost a shadow, flashed to Earline and slipped a long, curved claw through Sebille's bind, slicing it open with a purple-colored energy.

Light flared around Earline and her skin slipped

to the floor, empty. Then with a cackle of pure glee, she and the shadow disappeared.

Before we had time to wrap our minds around what had just happened, the massive snake blinked itself awake on a roar.

12

AGAIN!

"What in the world?"

Birte leaped into the air, bursting into the massive dragon and landing on the Naga's back, just behind its head. The dragon opened its jaws wide and clamped them over the snake's body.

The monster roared again, surging upward to buck against Birte's constraint.

Sebille ran toward the immobile giant, flinging herself to her belly to avoid being smacked with a flailing dragon wing. The snake swung sideways, its massive jaws opening and snapping inches from my face.

Grym punched a rock-hewn fist into the creature's snout, barely dazing it as Sebille climbed to her feet and ran toward Theo.

The snake's coils snapped sideways, trapping the Sprite against the bathroom door on a grunt of pain.

"Are you all right?" I screamed.

She lifted her hand, showing me the last piece of magicked cookie. "Here!"

With an internal groan, I lifted my hands to catch it.

The snake tried to roll over to lose the dragon.

The thick body smacked into me just as the cookie fell into my outstretched palm.

I yelped as the cookie went flying and screamed for Grym.

His blocky fist shot out and snatched the treasure from the air.

"Theo?" he asked.

I nodded and then remembered. "Half! We should give the snake some too. Maybe that will force him back to Devard."

Grym broke the sweet in half. "Give this to Theo at the same time."

I nodded, grimacing as the cookie piece left his hand and flew toward me. The chances of me even catching it were...

The cookie hit my palm and my fingers closed around it.

Pretty good, apparently.

I took off running. The snake surged forward, its cool breath bathing my neck as I kicked up my speed to keep from feeling its fangs against my skin.

With another roar, the Naga rose up on its coils, smacking Birte against the ceiling and sending dust raining down on our heads. The floor rumbled as they hit the ground again and sent me sprawling, arms scraping along the carpet. The cookie flew out of my hand. *Buzzard blinkers!*

Sebille sent green energy into the snake's thick body. It roared, jerking far enough away for her to drop to the ground and crawl out from under its writhing coils.

She ran toward me. "Where is it?"

I shoved painfully to my feet. "I don't know, it took a flyer."

Sebille and I crawled around on the ground, trying to dodge the snake and the dragon while looking for the magicked sweet. We couldn't find it.

I was starting to worry it had been crushed to dust beneath the Naga.

In the meantime, the snake continued to fight Birte's restraint. The massive head swung sideways, scooping me off my feet and flinging me toward the tree.

I hit the prickly branches and felt the sharp, metal posts of the artificial concoction biting into my skin. With a pain-filled yelp, I skidded down the branches and landed in a puddle on top of Lea's scarf.

A furry gray form flew through the air with an angry yowl, hissing as he landed on the snake's head.

"No!" I screamed as Wicked sliced his razor-sharp claws across the snake's snout.

With an enraged roar, the snake flung its head sideways, trying to unseat my cat.

Silvery light stabbed into the snake's slitted eyes, blinding it as Hex joined Wicked on the monster's head. The sigils on the two cats' chests glowed, and a haze of silver magic bathed the snake, momentarily disorienting it.

The snake rose into the air, weaving back and forth as if drunk, and then slammed to the ground and sent the cats flying. They landed on their feet a few yards away and then scampered toward the food covering the floor as if they hadn't just faced off with a prehistoric monster.

"Here it is!" Lea yelled, holding up the piece of cookie. She looked at Grym. "Now!"

The two of them shoved cookie into Theo's and the Naga's faces at the same time.

For a beat, nothing happened. Then Theo's eyes blinked open. He looked around the room, his gaze finding Birte struggling to keep the snake from rising off the floor again.

His protective instincts kicked in and Theo stepped into motion on a shout of pure rage.

The Naga convulsed, its shape wavering and stretching as it fought to get free. For a moment, I thought I saw Devard's face superimposed over the monster's snout and I knew he was fighting for control.

Charcoal-colored magic rose from the snake's

skin, settling down to twist around its glistening scales and slow its movements.

The magic wound around the Naga's head, coiling around its long body like two strings of macabre Christmas lights, and wrenched the snake upward, flinging Birte and Theo away.

Panic had me stepping forward. Fear that Devard was going to lose the battle and release the snake rather than imprison it had me shouting his name.

But the magic wrapped more tightly around the Naga, compressing its enormous body as it tightened. And when it was only six feet long and completely enmeshed in Devard's magic, it began to take a different form. Its smooth sides bent and reformed to the shape of a man. Its tail dividing into legs. Two arms rose from the scaly sides and Devard's features settled over the face.

Standing with bowed head and fisted hands, Devard shuddered once, violently, and then took a deep breath and opened his eyes. "Well, that was exciting."

Birte handed Devard a towel to wrap around his hips, her ruddy cheeks even redder than usual. She wore the tattered remains of the robe she'd been wearing when she shifted. I made a mental note to find something in my closet she could wear home.

Theo shrank back to his human-facing size.

We all collapsed into exhausted puddles of goo.

Lea looked at me, her face a study in weariness. "How about we never do this again?"

I gave her thumbs up in full agreement. "Thanks for your help," I told my friends.

"Sure, but next year I can't come," Devard said. "I have a...thing,"

I snorted out a laugh.

Lea looked at the skinsuits on the floor. "Skinwalkers?"

Grym frowned.

"It appears so," Sebille said. "Wait until I tell Mother."

"What's a Skinwalker?" I asked.

"They can shift into anyone or anything simply by conjuring a skin to match their target," Grym said. "But the kicker is, they take on all the attributes of the target while they're wearing the suit. They can use their magic, their knowledge, their memories, everything that makes the target what it is."

"Is the identity mixing spell part of their bag of tricks?" Lea asked.

Grym shrugged. "If the targets they're impersonating can perform that spell, then so can they."

"That's terrifying," I said.

He nodded. "And it makes it darn hard to catch them. The only chance we have is to find them in their base forms. They have very little inherent magic of their own."

"They must have crashed the party just to steal that box," Sebille said.

"But why?" Lea asked. "Certainly, they didn't do all this for a music box."

"More than a music box," Sebille said. "That box holds the essence of Christmas. Love, life, magic, within its frame. For someone who's having trouble embracing the spirit of the season, it can mean the difference between happiness or depression, life or death."

Grym sighed. "She's right. That box would fetch a pretty penny on the black market. We've been chasing a thievery ring for the last few weeks. We haven't been able to figure out how they get in and out without being seen. Now I know. They don't look like thieves. They look like the people who live in the target house."

"What are they stealing?" I asked. "They seemed to know exactly what they were looking for here. They were all over the library and didn't take anything. They just wanted the box."

"As far as I can tell, they're fencing magical arti-facts," Grym explained. "They target artifacts owned by non-magical people. We believe they get orders for items from specific buyers."

"Speaking of the box," I said, "where is it, anyway?"

"Here, Miss," Sitting atop the shelves, Hobs had the box clutched in his hand. "Is it time to open it?"

I glanced around Croakies, frowning at the devastated store and my worn out and slightly battered friends. I fought a wave of despair. "This isn't what the season is supposed to be about."

"Isn't it?" Sebille asked me, a gleam in her eye.

Grym placed a hand on my shoulder. "Are you sure?" he asked with a smile.

Birte and Theo walked over together, their hands clasped. Birte reached out and grabbed my hand, giving it a squeeze. "It was a fun adventure, Naida."

I glanced around. They were all smiling.

"Meow!" Wicked's soft, warm body wound between my legs and he sat on my feet. He started to bathe his legs, purring loudly.

"Ribbit!"

Slimy hopped across the floor, stopping beside Wicked and staring at my cat with his bulgy, blank eyes.

"The gang's all here," Theo said in his jolly, rumbling voice.

I snorted out a laugh. They were right. We were together. We were all safe. And together we'd created a Croakies kind of Christmas.

I shook my head. "You're all crazy. No wonder I like you."

Orchestral music throbbed through the room as the Soul of Christmas box continued to offer hope for a delightful and peace-filled holiday season.

Devard headed for the door. "I have a turkey and some other food at home. I'll be right back."

I watched him leave, emotion making my chest tight. "He's going to freeze his toogies off in that towel."

Sebille chuckled.

"I have pies." Lea followed him out.

"I need to go report this and set up a task force. Now that we know what we're dealing with, we can be more effective in finding the thieves," Grym said.

I nodded, thinking of the faint image in the Book of Pages. It suddenly made sense. The book had been trying to show me something that had no real likeness of its own. "Thanks for your help. Will you let me know when you find them?" I wouldn't rest entirely easy until I knew the skinwalkers were behind bars.

"Of course." He held my gaze for a long moment, his stare a question I wasn't ready to answer.

He wanted to know if I'd forgiven him, and I just wasn't sure.

After Grym left, I glanced toward the broken table and the food mess. "I guess we need to clean that up."

"I'll help," Sebille offered.

Theo was eyeing the ceiling. "I think I can bend those tiles back into shape." Bathed in a soft, yellow glow, he grew until he was tall enough to reach the thirty-foot-high ceiling.

Birte looked at me. "What do you want me to do?"

I glanced around. "Can you grab the vacuum? It's in the closet by the tea stuff."

Birte headed that way.

Sebille walked over and stood next to me. Together we eyed the wrecked tree with its shattered bulbs and tangled strands of lights.

I sighed. "Well, we tried."

Hobs appeared between us, giving each of us a hand. "Merry Christmas, Miss N and Miss S."

"Merry Christmas, Hobs," we said in unison.

Merry Christmas, a small voice said behind us. I turned and found Slimy staring blankly at the tree. I stared at him a moment, wondering. Had he? I shook it off. Nah. It couldn't have been. I was hearing things.

Hobs sighed wistfully.

Sebille and I shared a glance over the hobgoblin's head.

We eyed the busted table a few feet away, and a slow grin spread across Sebille's face.

With a joyful whoop, we lifted the little guy high in the air and threw him onto the table. We each grabbed a section of the sides and began pushing the table across the carpet, swinging it this way and that to fling Hobs from side to side. Hobs held on, shrieking with laughter as his scrawny body slipped wildly across its slippery surface.

We reached the end of the room and whipped it around, Hobs squealing with delight as he barely managed to keep hold of the table's edge. His skinny legs swung sideways, and Sebille and I whipped it back the other way, giggling breathlessly. Hobs was laughing so hard he could barely breathe.

Without warning, the table smacked into the bookshelves on either side, not quite wide enough for the table to fit down the aisle. The impact sent Hobs' small form flying off the table and tumbling through the air. He smacked into the back of the upholstered chair in the central reading area, disappearing from view as the chair fell backward with a thump.

There was a moment of expectant silence as we waited for him to show back up.

A spidery finger appeared on the edge of the chair seat. And another, and another, then a pair of large pointed ears, a shock of light-brown hair, and a pale, red-cheeked face.

Hobs' eyes were wide, sparkling with delight as he clapped his hands and screamed.

"Again!"

The End

AUTHOR'S NOTE

The holidays are a time to celebrate life, laughter, and love. A time for family, friends, good food, and fun activities. But they can also be a difficult time of year for people who don't feel the joy. My greatest hope, with this holiday story, is to give someone a sliver of happiness and wonder. Making someone smile is the stuff of true joy. I write my books in the hopes that they'll provide smiles and good feelings. I write because I want to make a difference in someone's life. I don't always achieve that goal. But I'm okay with that. If I make a few of you smile, or gasp, or even cry happy tears, I'll feel like I've done my job.

Merry Christmas, Happy New Year, and may you forever be blessed with the gift of laughter and love.

xx

Sam

READ MORE ENCHANTING INQUIRIES

Did you enjoy **Frosted Croakies**? If so, you might want to check out Book 7 of the *Enchanting Inquiries Paranormal Mystery series.*

Please enjoy Chapter One of Milk & Croakies, my gift to you!

Farmer Blue has lost his cows and doesn't know where to find them. But Farmer blue has found guess who, to wrangle the magic that binds them.

I'm really not much of a country mouse. Up until recently, my idea of the great outdoors has been Enchanted Park in the center of the city. But my job is to wrangle magical artifacts. So, when a local farmer calls to tell me his dairy cows are disappearing and he thinks it's the work of a rogue artifact...sigh...it appears I'm about to get a crash course in becoming a farm girl.

These cows haven't just meandered away chewing their cuds. They've actually disappeared.

Poof!

As in here one minute, gone the next. Which means it's up to me to don tall rubber boots and traverse the cow bumps...slog through the cow patties...and reach into the abyss to try to drag them back.

I'm not sure how the frog and the cat are going to help with this one. I really didn't want to bring them along at all. But you know how insistent they can be...

Wait...where's the frog? Has anybody seen my cat?

Slimy! Wicked! Where on earth have you gotten off to?

Poof?

MILK & CROAKIES

"Inside the tank of the Magic Muffin Maker," I told the little hobgoblin standing happily before me. With that pronouncement, Hobs' oversized ears drooped and took his smile with it.

"Horse halitosis," Hobs murmured.

I took up the smile he'd lost. "You can't beat me at this game, Hobs. I'm the queen of my domain."

Okay, maybe I was being a little cocky, but ever since I'd formally bonded with Croakies and the artifact library, I was a walking treasure map for everything inside the place.

Well, everything magical, anyway. I still couldn't find my car keys from that morning. I could swear I'd put them into my jacket pocket when I got back from the grocery.

"Jack's bag of magic beans," Sebille said.

"Inside the pocket of the giant's burlap trousers."

Sebille's face fell.

"The last red feather SB dropped," Hobs exclaimed gleefully.

Sebille gave him rock knuckles, and the two of them turned a united grin and a smug attitude in my direction.

I hesitated for effect, giving them a moment to enjoy their perceived victory. Then I opened my mouth to destroy their happiness. "Third shelf on the fifth shelving unit, center section. Next to the stack of Doctor Osvald's books." I squinted thoughtfully. "The book on top is entitled, *Six Magickal uses for Overripe Bananas and Avocados*."

The duo deflated like last winter's badly tied balloons.

"You're a derf," my lovely assistant informed me.

The front door to the bookstore opened. Lea came inside, frowning. "Hex's collar is miss..."

I pointed to the top of the nearest shelving unit. "It's up there."

"...ing," she finished, her frown deepening. "You know that's getting creepy, right?"

I laughed happily. I was enjoying my newfound skills too much to let them ruin it for me.

My phone rang and I answered with a chirpy, "Croakies Bookstore, Where Magic Happens."

Sebille rolled her eyes and Lea chuckled.

"Is this Naida Griffith, Keeper of the Artifacts?"

My chirpy happiness drained away. "Yes, this is Keeper Naida. Do you need help with an artifact?"

"I do. And it's an emergency."

I grabbed the Book of Pages, intending to call up his problem as he explained it to me. "What's happening?"

"Bessy's disappeared."

I nodded. "Okay, is Bessy your wife? Daughter? Girlfriend?"

"What are you, some kind of sicko?"

I blinked. "Um, no. I'm just trying to get some basic information so I know what I'm up against..."

"Bessy's my best producer. But she's more than that..." The man's voice turned gruff. He sounded like he was near tears. "She's kind of a friend, I guess."

"Can you describe her to me?" I asked, oozing efficiency. I wondered if Grym would be on the case. A missing person would be right up his alley.

The thought depressed me a little. We hadn't been speaking much lately. We'd had a...well... disagreement seemed too mild a term for it.

"Bessy's a hefty girl, with golden hair and soulful brown eyes."

I should really be writing everything down. "Does Bessy have any distinguishing characteristics?"

"Yeah, she's missing," the man on the other end of the line growled.

I bit back a growl of my own. "Can you describe what she was wearing when you last saw her? Clothing, jewelry?"

"Well, Bessy didn't wear too much clothes. But she had a giant brass bell around her neck."

Of course she did.

"So let me recap. I'm looking for a large, naked female with golden hair and soulful brown eyes, wearing a bell."

Sebille, Hobs, and Lea cackled and I had to shush them.

"Look, lady. I ain't never heard of no cows wearin' clothes, but if you think the lack of them clothes makes her naked, then fine. She's naked. Now, can you come out to the farm and look for her. I'm really startin' ta get worried."

I felt all the blood leave my face. "Farm?" My voice squeaked over the word. "You live on a farm?"

His silence was like a thousand Sebille eye rolls. "You didn't think I'd keep a cow in the city, did you?"

"Oh. Yeah. A cow." Did cows bite? Maybe I should bring SB and the sword with me.

I could almost hear the man frown. "You sure you're up to this? I'm startin' ta worry you ain't all there."

I sighed. "No. I'm good. If you'll just give me your address."

"Take the main road West outa town. Turn left at that big tree with the flaking bark and drive about three miles up the gravel road. We're the farm on the left with the giant cow statue upfront. You can't miss it."

Yeah, I was pretty sure I could. I thanked him and told him I'd be there as soon as I could, disconnecting as thunder rattled the windows. Rain beat against the glass, wind driving it so hard it sounded like hail.

"We get to go to a farm," I said with forced cheerfulness as I slid my phone into my pocket. Unfortunately, when I looked up, I discovered I was alone in the store.

The derks had run away at the first mention of vast, messy plots of land dotted with large and stinky domestic animals.

Maybe I shouldn't have been so smug about the feather thing.

There's really nothing magical about cow manure. Even when it's mixed into ankle-deep mud, forming an aroma that cannot be described without an entire volume of creative swears.

I tugged against the sucking pull of the muck, feeling my rubber boot slide away from my foot as I tried to lever it free.

I stopped, jamming my foot back down inside the boot.

"Ribbit!"

The only thing worse than traversing a muddy field in a driving rain was traversing the muddy field in a driving rain with a mouthy frog in my pocket.

"I'm well aware that there's a pond over there, Slimy. You're not going anywhere near it."

"Ribbit?"

I sighed. "Because I don't want to lose you. My luck, you'd jump into it and swim away, and I'd never find you among the lily pads and cattails."

"Meow!"

Miserable in the rain, Wicked shivered beside me, his usually tidy feet coated in slimy muck up to the ankles. I'd tried to carry him across the field, but he was having none of it.

I cast my hopeful gaze toward the small, white farmhouse in the distance. "Maybe you should just run ahead, Mr. Wicked. I'll get there as soon as I can."

Expecting my stalwart cat to refuse to leave me, I watched, shocked and mortally wounded as he took off with a yowl, leaving me in his proverbial dust.

Or muck.

"I see where your loyalties are, you little traitor!" I called after him.

Lightning flashed in the distance. A few seconds later, thunder boomed, seeming to shake the entire world by the roots.

"Ribbit!"

"I'm trying!" I yelled at the frog. I immediately regretted being so cross with the fat little amphibian. It wasn't his fault he was stuck in the middle of a muddy field with me.

I sighed. "Sorry, Slimy. I really wish your driver was on board, though. Maybe Rustin could figure out a way for us to get where we're going."

I missed Rustin for a lot of reasons. Since he'd gone, Slimy hadn't spoken a single word. Though I'd gotten really good at understanding his frog language. I'd thought the two of them had developed separate consciousnesses. The fact that Slimy seemed irreparably changed by Rustin's desertion bothered me. A lot.

I only hoped Rustin was faring better than the frog.

Another world-shaking boom forced me to a decision I knew I was going to regret. I slipped my feet out of the boots and took off running toward the house in my stocking feet.

Well, not running exactly. More like slogging faster without the boots to drag me down.

Mud squished through my toes and splashed up my leg. I grimaced at the slimy feel of it and prayed the sewer-like stench didn't soak into my skin. The last thing I needed was to end up smelling like a dumpster.

The rain turned torrential, pounding onto my soggy head like typewriter keys hitting paper. Lightning arced from the leaden sky, slamming into a tree a mere fifteen feet away. I screamed, my foot glancing off the edge of a water-filled cow bump, and fell over, my entire left side splashing into icy water.

That was the last straw. I had to change course.

I wasn't going to make it to the farmhouse.

I climbed to my feet and switched directions, heading toward the old barn in the near distance.

I hit the enormous sliding door at a run, palms slapping into the moist wood as I pressed closer in the hopes the ancient structure would protect me just by its nearness and sheer size. I shoved the door open just enough to squeeze through, and stood shivering in the silty dirt. It was drier inside the old wooden building than I'd assumed it would be. Quieter.

Lightning struck again and I jumped, squealing. The strike had sounded terrifyingly close.

Leaving the sliding door open a couple of feet to allow the dove-gray light of the overcast day inside, I moved further into the space, looking around.

The floor of the barn was dirt mixed with hay and wood shavings. The place smelled like fresh hay, the air sweet and surprisingly clean.

I hadn't expected that.

The other thing I hadn't expected were the inquisitive gazes of the cows. Gathered together in a large enclosure on one end, with a door to the field beyond, my bovine barn-mates chewed thoughtfully as they eyed my disheveled self. Their ears twitched flies away as they chewed, the tags showing white in the dim light.

I knew from my quick conversation with Farmer Blue, that he kept dairy cows. I looked around for the equipment he used to milk them and saw nothing but a few pitchforks and a couple of metal bins along the sidewall that I assumed were filled with grain.

The loft high overhead was filled with stacked green cubes of hay, and a wooden ladder attached to the loft seemed the only way to access the higher spot.

I looked longingly up at that sweet, clean hay and sighed. I was not a farm girl by any stretch of the imagination. But I'd always had a thing for haylofts and green, sweet-smelling hay.

I was oh so tempted to climb that ladder and take a nap in the soft hay. The strenuous activity had worn me out.

Yawning widely, I decided I needed a cup of Sebille's energy tea.

I shook my head. No, I'd wait by the door until the storm died down and then head for the house.

That plan lasted all of five minutes. The steel-gray clouds high above just kept coming. As one angry-looking bank of the things moved on past, it was replaced by another, even angrier looking bank.

I was clearly going to be in that barn for a while.

Shivering violently, I turned and looked longingly up at the loft, making a sudden decision. It would be warmer up there. Maybe there'd be an old horse blanket or something I could wrap myself up in. I'd just take a few minutes to rest my eyes and dry off.

Decision made, I looked down at Mr. Slimy, who'd been suspiciously quiet since our sprint to the barn. "You'll like the loft," I assured him happily. "I'm sure there will be lots of spiders and stuff for you to eat up there."

He fixed his blank, black gaze on me and puffed his throat unhelpfully.

Slipping him into the pocket of my jacket, I headed for the wooden ladder. I was eager to check out the loft and happy I'd found an excuse to do it.

A chilly breeze wafted through the door, and hay sifted down onto my head.

A muffled thumping rose above the cow enclosure. I peered down on them as I started climbing up the ladder, finding them still chewing and staring, their bovine heads lifting to follow my progress upward.

"Nothing to see here, girls," I told them. "These are not the drones you're looking for."

A clump of hay hit me in the face, some of it falling into my open mouth. "Ugh!" I spit it out, plucking at my tongue to remove some pieces that stuck there.

"Whathh in the worldth?"

The ladder wobbled, and I looked up in surprise. Footsteps pounded the rungs. Another clump of hay sifted over me.

I sneezed, my eyes closing for just a beat and when I reopened them I saw a face, just a flash of eyes with a greasy fringe of hair falling over a grungy face, and then something shoved my shoulders and I was suddenly sailing backward, toward the hard, dusty ground below.

Check out the entire series here: https://samcheever. com/books/#enchanting

ALSO BY SAM CHEEVER

If you enjoyed **Frosted Croakies**, you might also enjoy these other fun mystery series by Sam. To find out more, visit the **BOOKS** page at www. samcheever.com:

Reluctant Familiar Paranormal Mysteries
Yesterday's Paranormal Mysteries
Gainfully Employed Mysteries
Silver Hills Cozy Mysteries
Country Cousin Mysteries

ABOUT THE AUTHOR

USA Today and WSJ Bestselling Author Sam Cheever writes contemporary and paranormal mystery and suspense, creating stories that draw you in and keep you eagerly turning pages. Known for writing great characters, snappy dialogue, and unique and exhilarating stories, Sam is the award-winning author of 80+ books.

To learn more about Sam and her work, visit her at one of her online hotspots:
www.samcheever.com
samcheever@samcheever.com

www.ingramcontent.com/pod-product-compliance
Lightning Source LLC
Chambersburg PA
CBHW070556180626
46817CB00005B/1874